Secrets of My Suburban Life

Also by Lauren Baratz-Logsted

. . .

Angel's Choice
Me, In Between

Secrets of My Suburban Life

Lauren Baratz-Logsted

SIMON PULSE

New York London Toronto Sydney

SIMON PULSE
An imprint of Simon & Schuster Children's Publishing Division
1230 Avenue of the Americas, New York, NY 10020
Copyright © 2008 by Lauren Baratz-Logsted
All rights reserved, including the right of reproduction in
whole or in part in any form.
SIMON PULSE and colophon are registered trademarks
of Simon & Schuster, Inc.
Designed by Jessica Sonkin
The text of this book was set in Lomba Book.
Manufactured in the United States of America
First Simon Pulse edition January 2008
2 4 6 8 10 9 7 5 3 1
Library of Congress Control Number 2007928370
ISBN-13: 978-1-4169-2525-5
ISBN-10: 1-4169-2525-2

*For the nephews—Andrew Baratz and
Benjamin Logsted—with love and just because*

Secrets of My Suburban Life

Dear Dr. Marlowe,

As I'm sure you'll understand, due to the events of this past summer, I've decided it's best that my daughter and I leave the Upper East Side. We'll be moving to Danbury, CT, where Lauren will be attending the Waylord Academy. While it does not perhaps have the cachet of The Simmons School for Girls, and I would have preferred she not be exposed yet to coeducation, I know you'll appreciate that this move is best for all concerned. For my part, I understand you will not be able to refund my deposit on the coming year, and that's just fine. Consider it a substantial down payment on a new limo bus.

Warm regards,

Frank D'Arc

Frank D'Arc

From: FDA
To: SexGurl

I'm sure it must be a drag wearing uniforms every day—what a blow to your fashion individuality! Still, I'd love to see you in your uniform one day. I'll bet you are hot hot hot!

Dear Mom,

I can't stop wondering what it's like where you are. Can you see us down here? Do you know what we're up to? I think you must know. Somehow, you must. And if I'm right, then you know Dad has decided to move us from New York to Connecticut. And you must also know how nervous that makes me: being taken away from my friends, being taken away from the only life I've ever known. Dad thinks this is for the best. He keeps saying that. But I don't agree at all. Doesn't he realize how scared and nervous all of this change makes me? I wish you were here to tell Dad what to do. I wish you were here to tell me what to do. I wish you were here so we could each say "I love you" one more time.

Wishing you were here,
Ren

Omigod!

I can't believe my dad yanked me out of Simmons and now I have to go to Waylord. What kind of name is that? It sounds so . . . religious. Like someone-got-lost religious. Or someone-got-stoned religious. *Way lord, dude.* Whatever. It's definitely not Simmons. I mean, Simmons is at least a pretty decent mattress.

And now here I am, flying down the stairs, late. But isn't that good, being late? Doesn't that mean I'm fashionable? But I'm still late, which might not be so bad, since maybe I'll miss the bus. I cannot believe I have to take an honest-to-God yellow school bus to Waylord, which does not even have a limo service like Simmons, not even close.

The town provides bus service for kids who live in Danbury because it has to. Kids in the surrounding towns get driven by their parents. Even kids from just over the border in New York State, some of whom live closer to the school than kids in some parts of Danbury, have to get to school some other way.

Yes, I'm flying in my uniform and I kiss my dad on the cheek, even though I'm still mad at him for moving us here, because I still love him no matter what. And I'm waving good-bye to Mrs. Johnson, the woman my dad hired to cook and clean for us, grabbing the pancake she's about to put on a plate for me right out of her hand, taking a bite—aargh! Frozen!—and now I am sooo out that door.

I get on the bus. It is already nearly full. In the very back row, the coolest seats on the bus, where *I* should by all rights be sitting, there is an impossibly gorgeous blond girl. Next to her there is one of the most gorgeous guys I've ever seen. Across the aisle from them sits a much younger girl who looks a lot like the gorgeous guy; she has the same deep auburn hair and brown eyes. I suppose I could walk back and sit next to her, but I don't, because I am The New Girl, and, well, I am totally insecure about being The New Girl.

I know no one. I cannot believe this. I take a seat behind the bus driver.

My uniform—maroon jacket, white shirt, and dark plaid skirt and matching tie—sucks. Never mind the dark kneesocks.

These kids look like they don't know *InStyle* from *People*.

My life is a living hell.

And now I am in my first ever homeroom at Waylord, and my life is even hellier than it was on the bus.

It starts when the teacher gets to the *D*'s.

"Lauren D'Arc?" He peers over his black horn-rimmed glasses. These are back in style now, but you know looking at him that he's had his since they were not.

"That's Ren," I correct him.

"Why not Lauren?" he says, looking down at his attendance sheet. "It says here Lauren."

Well, then, it must be true, right? You literal idiot.

Of course, I can't say that.

And I also can't say, *Because Lauren used to be the coolest name in the world, when just about the only person in the world to have it was Bacall and she was blowing smoke rings in Bogey's face. But now Laurens are an AmEx Gold Card a dozen.*

The reason I can't say that is because, before even getting to the *D*'s, Mr. Welch had already called out four other Laurens, proving my point.

"It's just what I'm used to," I say, shrugging my shoulders. "It reminds me of my old home."

I know he will not question me on this further and that he will let me have my way with my name. I know this because the teachers at Waylord have all been briefed on the tragic events of my summer, and they will not want to upset me further. I know this because I know everything, not because I'm sneaky, but because I'm intuitive.

It's not the best of all worlds, getting your way because other people feel sorry for you. But if that's what it takes to have the name I want, I'll exploit now and guilt later.

"Ren D'Arc," Mr. Welch says. "Your father is the famous writer."

I nod, looking at my desk, hoping he will guess I don't want to talk about it.

I could also tell him that the name used to be Dark but that my mother thought it was too, well, *dark*. So we changed the spelling but not the pronunciation. Except I don't want to talk to him about my mother, either.

While he has been going down the attendance sheet, I've been putting the names together with the faces, trying to figure out which of the girls would make a good friend. The boys—which ones I might want to date, which ones I should avoid—I can sort out later. For now I need to find a girlfriend.

But so far the prospects are absent.

Then he gets to the *F*'s and Farrin Farraway.

I recognize her right away, with her blond hair cut like a knife. She is the impossibly gorgeous girl I saw on the bus. She is who I used to be at Simmons; well, except for the impossibly gorgeous part. She is the most popular, the one who fashion follows rather than she following it. She is also, clearly, a total bitch. Even when I was at the top of the food chain, I was never that.

"Got any tips from your father for us on the market?" Mr. Welch asks her.

"You should know SEC rules prevent my answering that," Farrin says.

And I think: *Typical. She wants to keep all the money for herself.*

I think: *No way will Farrin and I ever be friends.*

I do pull up short when Mr. Welch calls out "Jack Nicholas" and I see what that name is attached to: the gorgeous guy who was sitting next to Farrin on the bus, a totally gorgeous guy with thick auburn hair, warm brown eyes, an athlete's hands, and a tie tied just loosely enough that you can tell he knows how to have a good time.

Wow, does he know how to slouch in a chair. I picture myself getting up from my own chair, taking that short sultry walk from *D* to *N*, settling down into his lap, and wrapping my loving arms around him.

I will get back to Jack Nicholas later, of that I am sure.

Mr. Welch gets to the *R*'s.

"Kiki Rodriguez?"

The girl he calls is beautiful, her skin and hair to die for.

"Is your mother really dead," Mr. Welch asks Kiki, "or is Nikos keeping her, not in a coffin, but frozen in the deep-freeze room of his subterranean cave?"

Even I understand his crass question. Kiki is the spitting image of her mother, Lili Rodriguez, whom *Soap Opera Digest* refers to as "the Carmen Electra of daytime TV." Lili is the star of my favorite soap, *All My Days of Restless Passion*, which is part conventional soap and part vampire drama. Occasionally, there's a witch.

"I'd be violating my mother's contract if I answered that," Kiki says.

And I think: *Maybe. Maybe she can be my friend.*

Finally, Mr. Welch gets to the *Z*'s.

"T'Keyah Zekiel?"

Even sitting down, you can tell she's taller than just about everybody in the room, definitely taller than Mr. Welch. She's also black and—at the risk of sounding trite—beautiful.

"Are the Knicks going to go all the way this year?" Mr. Welch asks her.

And now I know who she is—of course I do. Her father, Isaiah Zekiel, is the greatest forward the Knicks have ever had. Her mother, Lucinda Schwartz, is arguably the only model who ever lived who is both blond and Jewish.

I look over at her, wondering: *Can she really live in Danbury?*

She must feel my eyes on her because her head snaps in my direction before I can look away. She stares. I know what she's seeing: I have dark hair too, but mine is straight, not a kink in sight. My eyes are brown, my skin is clear, my breasts are out of proportion to my waist, and even sitting down, you can tell I'm probably the shortest person in the room.

Since I've been caught staring, I give a little wave.

Slowly, she smiles. Then she turns back to Mr. Welch.

"Hey," she says, that smile still there, only now it's different, "you don't ask me about my dad and I won't ask you about your wife. Deal?"

As the room laughs, I look at her and I think, *That's her. She will be my new best friend.*

From: FDA
To: SexGurl

I don't think age matters very much where matters of the heart—not to mention other things—are concerned, do you? You seem to be very mature for your age. And, well, sometimes I am very immature for mine. Perhaps we are perfectly matched?

Dear Mom,

It is sooooo much worse than I thought. I used to think that people are the same everywhere, but now I think that that's only because wherever I went before, I was always with the same kind of people. Maybe I'm not explaining this too clearly. I'll try to do better.

It's like this, I think: Back home, in New York—I don't think I'll ever think of Connecticut as home—I understood the rules. Everyone at Simmons strived for a certain . . . way of being. But here that doesn't work for me. It's as if what was perfect before—the right hair, the right clothes, the right makeup—is now too much of a good thing, and that somehow makes it a bad thing. Sure, most of the kids at Waylord are as rich as the kids at Simmons, but it's a different kind of rich: It's a suburban, rather than a city, rich. And did you see where I wrote "most of the kids"? It seems some of the kids at Waylord are on financial aid. And some of the other kids seem to look down on them for this, even though they don't say anything out loud. Not really.

Oh, and there's this one boy—if you were here, I would tell you all about him—who is just too gorgeous to be believed. His name is Jack Nicholas. There is something very "real" about him, if you know what I mean, but I guess that doesn't matter much since Farrin Farraway seems to have a history with him. Nobody has really said as much to me—hell, no one has really talked to me yet—but I just sense it.

Anyway, I am trying to make the most of things, and I am hoping to make at least one friend here, preferably before I graduate. It has been two weeks since I have received an e-mail from Shannon, even though I have written her several times in between. Do you think she has forgotten all about me?

Wish you were here,
Ren

Being a writer killed my mother.

No, it's not what you think. She didn't die from an exploding computer or have a heart attack because J. K. Rowling kept making the bestseller lists when she didn't. It wasn't anything like that.

Actually, J. K. Rowling *did* kill my mother.

No, it's not what you think. She didn't come over here from Scotland or England or wherever she lives and stab her in her sleep or put arsenic in the new paint. It wasn't anything like that.

Like my dad, my mom is—*was*—a writer.

People used to think it must be the most amazing thing, having two writers for parents. And it was. In a way. Our house in New York had this incredible staircase, wide with red carpeting going up to a landing where it split off in two directions to the top floor. Dad used to write on the left side, Mom on the right. At the end of the workday they'd both emerge, meet in the middle, and walk the rest of the way down holding hands. Then they'd go into the library, where they'd share an expensive bottle of wine while taking turns reading each other the day's new pages.

At least that's the way I remember it.

And it was pretty great, being the daughter of two writers, except that they both expected I'd one day want to write too, which is just a bad idea all around.

My writing sucks.

But it was still pretty great until the day J. K. Rowling killed my mother.

Mom was doing research for a new book she was working on. It was a comic mystery with a very strange setup, kind of like the reverse of a pyramid. It started out with ten characters, all having some kind of glamorous career, none of the characters seeming to have anything to do with the others. At the end of each chapter one of the characters dies. Gruesomely. You don't even want me to tell you about the free razor blade one guy got in the mail, with the tip laced with poison from a South American dart frog.

Anyway, Mom was working on the chapter where the novelist gets it in the end. She had the idea that it would be some kind of ironic justice if this bestselling author was killed by her own lousy books. So she figured she'd have her character stage a publicity event before a book signing. A delivery truck was supposed to deliver thousands of the author's books to the Barnes & Noble on the Upper West Side. The back door would slide up, the books would be balanced on the freight elevator, and the novelist would crouch underneath, like a female Atlas dressed in a pink tweed suit holding up the world. In the book the killer was supposed to have paid the truck driver, whose kid had an expensive Game Boy obsession, to screw around with the freight elevator so that it would malfunction, crushing the novelist.

But my mom, being the kind of stickler for research she was, just had to try the stunt out for herself. So she offered a real truck driver money so she could see what it would feel like to crouch under there, all that weight poised dangerously above her. And, of course, life imitating fiction as it always does, the freight elevator really did malfunction.

The coroner said that if it had been one of the earlier Harry Potter books, the thinner ones, she might've survived. But, as it was, it was one of the later fat ones, and a thousand of those babies, crashing down on Mom's pretty head, was enough to take her away from me for good.

People think it's hard when your parents divorce. Well, I don't know about that, since that's never happened to me. I'll tell you one thing, though: I'd rather have divorced parents than have one of them be dead.

But I'm not looking for the sympathy vote for my mom dying young and beautiful, although God knows I miss her.

And I'm not looking for the sympathy vote for my mom dying for her art, even though I miss her every day.

I'm looking for the sympathy vote because, in the wake of her tragic death, *my father decided to move us to Danbury!*

This is the worst of all possible worlds because:

1. It is not Manhattan.
2. It is not Manhattan.
3. I do not know how to drive.

In Manhattan not driving is not a teenage tragedy. In Manhattan people don't drive. People from outlying areas, foolish people, might drive *to* Manhattan, but nobody drives *in* Manhattan. Yes, yes, I know, when you go to Manhattan, you see lots of cars everywhere, bumper-to-bumper traffic; but nearly everyone you see driving is being paid to drive. Believe me when I say this: You do *not* see people hopping into the Jeep Cherokee to pick up a quart of soy milk at the nearest grocery store.

It had been my plan to spend my entire life not

driving a car. My mother and father, both native New Yorkers, had never learned how to drive. If it was good enough for them . . .

But now I am living in Danbury, in can't-get-there-from-here-*unless-you-drive-a-car* Danbury, and I am stuck.

When we first moved here a few months ago, my dad had what *he* thought would be this great idea: We would both learn to drive over the summer!

For himself, he did just fine with the lessons, even if he did dent the front fender of the driving school car a bit when he tried to pull back into our driveway, plowing down the mailbox along the way. For myself . . . I was terrified!

But I couldn't tell him that. How uncool would that be? *Um, Dad? The idea of coordinating all that stuff with the brakes and the gas and the gears and the wheel just scares the shit out of me! And what do I do when I need gas for the damn thing? All I see around this damn town are self-service pumps!*

So, after my first and last driving lesson—a lesson during which all I did successfully was turn the key in the ignition, listen to the engine purr, and tell Mr. Welky, "Wow, that thing sure does hum. Well . . . thanks!"—I told my dad a creative truth.

"This is a dangerous idea you have," I said, helping

myself to the turkey and mashed potatoes Mrs. Johnson made. "I'm too young to be driving a car."

My dad, sitting at the head of the long table in his heavy mahogany chair in the forest green dining room, dropped the ladle in the silver gravy boat as though I'd said something really startling, like that Mark Twain was just a hack with a weird sense of humor or that Stephen King should get the Pulitzer or something.

"You're too young to . . . what?" He shook his head, as though there were a fly in his ear. "You're not too young to dress like you're twenty-five when you want to. You're not too young to smuggle my wine into school to get the whole class drunk." Oh. I guess he knew about that. And here I thought the headmistress of Simmons was being cool about it and that she'd keep her word when she said that if the responsible parties came forward—which turned out to be Shannon and me—there would be no repercussions. Oh, well. At least now I know why my parents sent me for psychiatric counseling for a whole month to discuss my alcohol issues. And here I thought it was because they'd found the bottle of peach schnapps in the back of my closet—the one that Shannon gave me for my last birthday; the one that I never even opened because I didn't even like to drink anymore, not after getting so sick the day of the wine smuggling. "You're not too young to do any of those things," he said, running his hand unconsciously through his light brown hair, what's left of it, that's been unconscionably thinning on him, his green eyes curious behind his silver-rimmed reading glasses. (I got my own nearly black hair, dark eyes, shortness, and 20/20 vision from Mom.) "But you're too young to learn how to drive a car? But it's not hard, honey. Even I learned."

Just barely, I thought but didn't say, thinking of the fresh dent in the blue Lexus now parked in our driveway.

"But I am too young!" I said. "It's only like I'm just one!"

"Huh?" he said.

Well, who can blame him?

"Oh, sure," I said, "I'm sixteen in New York years, which actually makes me about eighteen in New Jersey years or twenty-two in Tennessee years, but really only maybe fourteen in Paris years."

"Huh?" he said again.

I ignored his confusion. Honestly, if he couldn't figure all of that out . . .

"But I'm only one in Danbury years!" I said. "I just got here. Stop rushing me!"

"Ohhh-kayyyy," he said, speaking real slow, like

maybe he was scared of ruffling the loony. "So, if you're not going to drive yourself, how are you going to get around? I mean, I know you have to take the bus to school anyway, because kids aren't allowed to have cars on campus and there's no point in my driving you when they have a perfectly good bus service. But what about other stuff? What about extracurriculars? What about going to the movies? What about *shopping*?"

"No worries," I said, taking a bite of my turkey. "I've got it all figured out."

"Oh, well, then, that's okay, I guess," he said, picking up the ladle again. Then he stopped, the ladle poised over his mashed potatoes. "Wait a minute," he said. "Just exactly *what* have you figured out?"

"How to get around Danbury or wherever I need to go," I said, chewing some more.

"And that is . . . ?"

"I'll call cabs."

But it's not as easy as I thought it would be, getting cabs in Danbury. The first time I tried to hail one several weeks ago, walking down our driveway to the street and holding my hand up in the air as if I were outside the Met and I wanted to go to Bloomies instead, was the first time I noticed, really noticed, that cabs do not just drive around aimlessly in residential Danbury, waiting to get flagged down. Hell, they don't even ride aimlessly around the busiest parts of the small city, waiting to get hailed. Oh, no. Nothing so practical as that, I fast learned. You have to *call* them, like calling a car service in New York. But worse than the inconvenience of having to look up the number or dial information every time you want to go somewhere (until you grow smart enough to program them into the speed-dial function on all of your phones, including your cell) is that once you have called them, then you have to *wait* for them.

I have come to learn, through many trials and much tribulation, that the Danbury taxi service I use, a terribly named business called Wheels Instead of Heels, does not have sufficient respect for the value of my time. I know this because whenever I call, the dispatcher says a cab will be wherever I am calling from in five to ten minutes. In fact, it was five to ten minutes only once, just one time. Every other time it has been at least fifteen minutes and sometimes as much as a whole hour. This makes it hard for me to plan things and also explains why when I went to the revival theater I had no idea that Nemo's mother was dead until the end of the movie, a fact I wish I'd known earlier so I could properly prepare myself, having assumed Marlin and her to be merely separated or divorced. Or maybe she just didn't care that her kid was missing. Or maybe, even, she'd run off with a cute shark who had a really big, um, fin.

Okay, I guess I was a bit out of it that night too.

For a while I tried overcompensating. I would call for a cab an hour before I had to be somewhere. But those were, of course, the times the cab would come in just fifteen minutes. And since I hate being too early to places, that wouldn't do either. So now I just wing it, never sure when I will get to a place.

My life is such a crapshoot!

I know I could call a company other than Wheels Instead of Heels—there actually are a few others in the phone book, and I have tried them all at least once— but I know I would not get the same personalized service and reliability. Oh, I don't mean in terms of promptness. As I think I've well documented here already, their promptness sucks.

No, by "reliability and service," I mean I like it that I always get the same drivers. If it is before six o'clock at night, I always get George, a middle-aged African American with a goatee and a lisp, who told me that airport security made his wife take off her underwire bra to inspect it for bombs or incendiary devices when it made the alarm go off at the checkpoint the last time she went to visit their daughter in Jacksonville. George's daughter is a lawyer, specializing in election law, which George says has become very lucrative in that part of the country. George works, not because he has to, but more because he doesn't have any hobbies. If it is after six o'clock at night, I always get Mohammed, who is short and wears one of those Middle Eastern head coverings. Mohammed does not want to be a cliché in America, so even though he has a cousin who said he could buy into his dollar-store business, he does not want to do that. He would rather make it on his own. He says if he can make it here, he can make it anywhere. When Mohammed drives me to the Danbury Fair Mall at night, I usually wear my pink wicker cowgirl hat with the rhinestone tiara decoration and Mohammed always says, "Nice hat," to which I always say, "Nice hat," to which he always says, "Wanna switch?" and we always do, but just for a minute. Mohammed says I am not like any American he has met yet. I think he means this as a compliment. And if I call on the weekends, I always get a woman who says to call her Blue. Blue is an Amazon, at least six feet tall, and has orange-red hair. Frankly, she scares me, so I try not to call on weekends.

But I like knowing I will get the same people, like knowing that at least George and Mohammed like to get me right back. And I tip well, so everyone's happy.

No, I don't blame the drivers for the lack of prompt-ness. I blame the dispatcher, a woman named Helena. She is always cranky when I call, and even though I have tried to politely explain that not knowing if the cab will come in fifteen minutes or forty-five minutes wreaks havoc with my social planning, I am positive she overbooks the drivers on purpose. I am also positive, even though I have never seen Helena, that she has a mole growing out of her chin that has a single long black hair sprouting from it and that she wears only double-knit polyester.

But it is not the weekend now, and it is after six, so I know Mohammed will be coming to get me when I call. And the reason I have to go out on this Monday night is because of the fucking Waylord Academy rules about sports.

This afternoon, in my first ever gym class there, I failed to distinguish myself as an athlete. We were on one of Waylord's many playing fields, the one that has a huge sloping hill edging one side of it. We were doing archery. Or, at least, we were all *supposed* to be doing archery.

I hung back, letting the others go first. Okay, I'll admit it: I wasn't hanging back to be polite. I was hanging back because I had no idea what I was doing. I mean, come on. It's not like there are lots of opportunities for using a bow and arrow in New York City.

I watched as T'Keyah, obviously the star athlete of the class, stood in position, one leg in front of the other, not shivering at all in her white T-shirt and maroon shorts because the day was so warm. I watched as she nocked the arrow, pulled back, let it fly; watched as it nailed that red spot clean in the middle. Then I watched as Kiki and several other girls came pretty damn close. Finally, Farrin, who seemed to be waiting me out to see which of us would be the coolest by going last, shrugged her shoulders, gave me a little sneer, and took her turn. Unlike everyone else, who had their T-shirts tucked neatly into their shorts or hanging out loose, Farrin had tied hers up high in a knot, right under her breasts, like maybe she was planning to go tan her flat abs at the beach later. Her blond hair was tied back in a loose ponytail—why can't I ever get my ponytails to look that nonchalant?—that seemed to seductively whisper to any guy who wandered past, *Rip me out.* (That would be the scrunchie holding her hair together doing the talking.) *Rip me out and throw me down in the tall grass over there, you . . . you . . . you you you* man, *you.* Farrin is just one of those kinds of girls whose scrunchie says a lot.

But getting back to archery.

Even though Farrin's form was nowhere near as perfect as T'Keyah's, and even though her face looked like she couldn't care less about what she was doing, bored, like she'd much rather be doing anything, even reading about Justin Timberlake, when she let fly that arrow, it was as true as T'Keyah's had been.

At last it was my turn. By now I was thinking, *How hard can this be?* I'd watched all the others. I thought I'd been paying attention.

I got into the position I'd seen the others stand in. I nocked the arrow. All the while I was thinking, *This is my chance to impress T'Keyah.* Ever since that morning, when I'd decided she would be my new best friend, I hadn't really had the chance of any contact with her. But now I did, and I was going to make the most of it. I'd nail that red spot like Farrin had, even better than Farrin had, and T'Keyah would be sure to see we were meant to be close friends.

I let the arrow fly.

Only it didn't fly.

It bulleted its way into the ground, only about two feet from where I'd shot it.

Farrin started to snigger. "Hey, D'Arc," she said, "if the earth ever tries attacking you, it doesn't stand a chance."

"I'm just getting . . . warmed up," I said.

I nocked another arrow. We were each supposed to get three shots per turn. I figured I had two more shots to make an impression; preferably, a good one.

"Aim a little higher," the gym teacher, Ms. Flick, called. Ms. Flick, with her short brown self-cut hair, her big-eater roll protruding through her polo shirt over the waistband of her gym shorts, her clipboard in her hands, her whistle around her neck, and her legs that look like they could crush coconuts *and* Mick Jagger between her thighs, looks like every gym teacher you've ever seen rolled into one, including the male teachers. She was standing halfway up the hill, off to the side of the target.

I lifted the bow and arrow, aimed high.

My eyes followed the shot arrow up, up, up, lost it in the sun, caught it finally coming downward, so far past the target that it landed in the woods.

"This isn't golf, D'Arc," Farrin said.

I wanted to say, *Oh, shut up,* but I thought that would make me seem even less dignified than I already felt.

I let the last arrow fly, my last big chance for the day.

Everyone laughed as Ms. Flick hit the ground on her stomach, just as the arrow whistled viciously over her head.

"Well, at least it went straight that time," Kiki said hopefully.

"Yeah," Farrin added with a laugh, "if only Flick were the target and not a hundred feet *away* from the target."

"Sports aren't exactly your strong suit," T'Keyah said, "are they?"

"Well," I said, "I guess I'm not very good at archery—"

"You suck at it," Farrin said, but I ignored her.

"—but I wouldn't say that sports per se aren't my strong suit," I went on.

"Oh," Farrin said, pretending to fluff her hair, "*per se*. Well, la-di-da."

"Never mind, Farrin," Ms. Flick said, coming up on the group with renewed confidence now that she was sure I didn't have any more arrows. "Listen up, people. Just because D'Arc isn't good at archery, it doesn't mean she sucks at all sports. Here at Waylord we believe that *everyone* has their strengths, however small those strengths might sometimes be. And, of course, as you all know, you each have to pick at least one sport. As in, right now. Sheets are posted outside the locker room already. Be sure to put your names down once you've changed," she said, then dismissed us.

What? What was she talking about?

"What's she talking about?" I grabbed T'Keyah's arm to hold her back as the others straggled on toward the field house and the locker room.

"You don't know?" she asked.

"Know what?" I said.

"About mandatory sports at Waylord. The damn school's so small that in order to have teams, everyone has to go out for at least one sport."

Crap! This place was nothing like Simmons. I'd no more go out for a team at Simmons than I would wear a skirt from last season's runway shows in Paris and Milan.

T'Keyah looked me up and down. "But I can see that's going to be a problem for you," she said.

Hey! I resented that! There was nothing wrong, nothing completely unathletic about the way I looked. She must have just been thinking about what she'd just witnessed me do at archery, and, okay, yeah, I really did suck at that.

"I have my . . . *talents*," I said, chin high.

"Such as?" She laughed. It definitely wasn't a mean laugh, not like Farrin's, but I had to admit that it was probably directed more at me than with me.

By now we were back at the field house, standing in front of the locker room, and T'Keyah wasn't even waiting until after showering and changing to decide what sport she wanted to try out for. She was scanning the sign-up sheets, looking for something. And then her eyes lit up. I watched as she took the marker that was hanging from the sheet and printed her name at the top underneath the word "BASKET-BALL."

"Basketball," I said defiantly, grabbing hold of the swinging marker she'd let go and writing my name under hers.

"Huh?" she said. Now it was her turn to be surprised.

"My talent," I said, "is basketball."

She looked down at me. She must have been at least a foot taller than me. Then a slow smile spread on her face.

"Oh," she said softly, "I think this is going to be good."

Why do I want T'Keyah to be my best friend so badly?

Because I respond to her sharp wit, particularly when it's directed at others. Because she's the only one who talks to me kind of regularly even if she does tease me a lot. Because she was the only one to smile at me in homeroom on the first day.

Hey, sometimes a girl's gotta take what a girl can maybe get.

From: FDA
To: SexGurl

I know this will sound strange, but my most fulfilling fantasies revolve around literary heroines. How about you? You probably fantasize about movie stars and rock stars. I guess it's too much to ask that you'd feel the same about this. How do you feel about Hamlet? Or maybe Huck Finn?

From: Shannongirl@yaahoo.com
To: RenD@aaol.com

Hey, R!

Long time no talk! Or write, I guess I should say. Listen, I've been
getting your e-mails, and I'm really sorry I haven't written back in
a while. But I'm sure you can imagine: Things are just soooo hectic
here! School started. Did it start for you yet? And you'll never guess
who's throwing a party already this weekend . . . Sheila Wentworth!
Listen, I know it's not like you two were ever friends, but maybe you
could come to it . . . as my guest? I'm pretty sure Todd'll be there. . . .

Anyway, gotta run! Mom's taking me shopping tonight for a
new outfit for the party. I want to get something black, but she's
resisting. "Any more black," she says, "and people will think you're
a mortician." Can you believe it???

Talk soon!
Luv,
S

I know absolutely nothing about basketball.

No, that is a lie.

I know exactly two things about basketball:

1. T'Keyah's father is one of the most famous basketball players, ever.
2. T'Keyah has clearly inherited her father's love of the game.

"Do you know anything about basketball?" I ask Mohammed when he picks me up that night. He is only twenty minutes late, which is very good, since I planned ahead. Since this night is so important to me, I called Helena ten minutes earlier than I normally would, so now I will be only ten minutes late. I guess I could have asked my dad about basketball, since he is, after all, a guy. But he'd probably just tell me to look it up in the encyclopedia or go watch a few games as research, and I don't have time for that. Plus, since Mom died, Dad and I barely talk. It seems like he spends every available minute, when he's not sleeping or eating, on the computer. I swear, it's like he lives on that thing now.

I see Mohammed shrug in the rearview mirror. "There is a ball. There is a hoop." He shrugs again. "It is kind of like golf, but without the cup, and it is in the air, not on the ground. Otherwise, it is the very same thing, yes?"

"Um, yes, I guess so," I hesitantly agree. "You play golf?" I ask.

"No. But how hard can it be?" Mohammed's third shrug. "Seems like the same as basketball to me, only it is outside, not in."

I decide that, for giving me athletic reassurance, I will tip Mohammed even more tonight.

"Why do you ask, Miss Ren?" he asks, pulling up in front of the field house. "Are you planning on playing golf in there tonight?"

"No, um, basketball. And I'm worried, because I've never played it before."

"Oh, don't worry, Miss Ren, you'll be fine."

I hand him yet another extra five for being my therapist.

"Just do not forget," Mohammed warns, "keep your eye on that tin cup."

As I get out of the taxi, I hear Farrin's laugh. "Nice wheels," she says.

Farrin is leaning against the field house, smoking. It is against Waylord rules to smoke anywhere on the grounds, not even teachers or parents are allowed, but people like Farrin always find a way around rules. Like by, say, just flouting them.

"*You* play basketball?" I ask, ignoring her remark.

"No," she says, looking down at her flippy maroon and white skirt and matching top before blowing smoke at me. She has on bright blue eye shadow and Egyptian-looking eyeliner, dark lipstick. "Do I *look* like I'm here for basketball? I'm here for cheerleading. You guys get one half of the court for your tryouts, we get the other." She takes another drag off her cigarette, holds it. "You're late," she accuses.

"Well . . . so are you," I counteraccuse, not able to think of anything more original to say.

"No, I'm not," she says. "I'm the squad captain."

If it is possible to suck more at basketball than I do at archery, then I suck more at basketball than I do at archery.

And more people than I would care for are there to witness my defeat. Apparently, the boys, Jack Nicholas among them, whose tryouts follow directly after the girls', are in the habit of arriving early, lolling around the bleachers while they observe. They tell Ms. Flick, who is engineering the whole thing by making sure everyone is where they are supposed to be, that they are hoping to pick up some tips on how to execute the soft touch by watching the girls. I know this to be bullshit because I can see what parts of the girls' anatomy their eyes are focused on as the girls run all over the court, and it is obvious that the tips and soft touches they are most interested in have nothing to do with basketball at all.

But this is no time for breasts.

No, this is no time for breasts, because the coach of the girls' basketball team has us doing laps around our half of the gym, and I am the slowest one here; because now she has us doing layups, and when I get under the basket and release the ball, it gets only halfway up to the net; because now she has us shooting from the foul line, and whenever I throw the ball, it makes it only halfway to the basket; because now she has us playing an actual mini-game, with man-to-man defense.

Or should I say T'Keyah-to-Ren defense?

I think that maybe I would have a chance at this game if the girl I was playing one-on-one with wasn't a foot taller than me. Every time I try to shoot over her, she slams the ball back toward my face. Every time she tries to shoot over me, she doesn't have to really try at all, her feet barely leaving the floor as she jumps, swishing that ball right in.

The coach finally realizes what a mismatch this is, and she has me switch places with another girl, puts me on T'Keyah's side. I think, *Great. This is my big chance. I will distinguish myself as being invaluable to her.*

But when she passes the ball to me, she throws it so hard, I feel the wind get knocked right out of my stomach—*whoosh!*—and I wind up flat on my back on the floor. She has to reach a hand down to me, help me to my feet.

By now cheerleading tryouts, which are supposed to be going on at the other end of the court, have ground to a halt. Everyone—those who are already on the team wearing their flippy uniforms and those who are hoping to make the team in their gym clothes—is watching me be a disaster, as are the boys in the bleachers.

"I think you need to be standing, if you want the ball to reach the basket," one guy shouts.

I recognize him from homeroom as being Michael Houseman; people combine the first initial of his first name with part of his last name and just call him Mouse. Mouse has longish blond hair and red-rimmed green eyes, making for a kind of weird Christmas motif, and I think he must be Waylord's biggest stoner. If, after this evening, I am too depressed to live, I know where I will go to buy drugs.

"Or you could just lie on the floor all day," the guy next to Mouse shouts. I remember his name is Dylan Zimmerman. He is very short, his brown hair cut in a way that makes it look like his mom made him do it like that, and I think he is Mouse's sidekick; or maybe not sidekick—more like the little dog that runs around the big dog's feet in a cartoon, panting and begging to be noticed. "You look better lying down than standing up," Dylan yells.

I ignore Dylan. I ignore everybody. And I *particularly* ignore Farrin Farraway, who is sneering for all she is worth at midcourt.

This is my last chance, I realize, this really is my last chance, as T'Keyah throws me the ball one last time, and—hey!—this time I catch it.

I am so surprised at this minor success, it takes me a while to orient myself. Which way is our basket? Oh, yeah, over there. I take off running toward it, remind myself I have to keep dribbling the damn ball or else.

For once I seem to be the fastest person here. It is like I am flying, leaving everyone else in my dust. I am hoping, praying, that if I make it to the basket, *when* I make it to the basket, I will finally be able to make the easy layup.

I am there now, I am almost right there, when my foot sticks to something on the floor. I watch my own body in horror as the unstuck foot keeps going forward, expecting the other foot to follow after, but the stuck foot remains behind. I watch in even more horror as the forward foot starts to slide, sliding, sliding, until I am forced into a perfect split. I have never done a split in my life, and it feels as though two giants have yanked my legs apart until they are almost ripping.

Well, I tell myself, *at least I am still holding on to the ball.*

But when I try to move, it is as though I am frozen in this position. It's like someone has glued me here.

I am the object of scorn. I begin to think that I will spend the rest of my life in this position. I picture graduation day a couple years down the road. Even if it is a beautiful day, with gorgeous weather, they will have to hold it right here in the gym to accommodate The Girl Who Got Stuck to the Floor.

Finally, I hear footsteps on the court, I see two large feet come to rest in front of me. I look up: It's T'Keyah.

"You don't really play basketball, either, do you?" she says. It's not like she's accusing me, more like she's just making a statement of observable fact.

I shake my head with the obvious: *No*.

She takes the ball out of my hands, practically has

to pry it loose from my grip, bends down, and rolls it gently off to the side. Then she takes both my hands in hers, hauls me to my feet. It's like I'm a rubber doll, my legs rising and coming together again without the knees bending at all.

"Well," she says, "you have to play some kind of sport: Waylord rules." She thinks about what to do with me for only a second before placing her hand on the small of my back and gently shoving me across the midcourt line. "She's all yours," she says to Farrin.

"All mine?" Farrin says, shoving me back across the line. "But I don't want her."

"All yours," T'Keyah insists, shoving me across one last time. "Hey," T'Keyah adds, as though I am not even there, "at least you know she can do a split."

And for the next hour I do whatever Farrin tells me to do. I do little leaps in the air. I memorize a few cheers and yell, "Yea, Panthers!" on cue along with everyone else. I force my body into split after split.

My cartwheels suck, so Farrin finds something else for me to do whenever the others are doing those, like, say, fetching her water. Farrin says that because I am shorter than everybody else, I can be on top of the pyramid. I do not tell her that I hate heights, but I do, particularly wobbly heights.

All the while I tell myself that this is okay. I tell

myself that even though I didn't make the basketball team, I impressed T'Keyah with what *Seventeen* calls my "sticktoitiveness." It's a hard sell, particularly since T'Keyah is no longer paying any attention to me whatsoever, but I tell myself that anyway.

I am outside at ten of nine, my knees bruised, my pride bruised. There is one other person outside in the dark: Jack Nicholas. He has on his basketball uniform, and he looks so jockily sexy, his legs strong, his arms strong. I smell smoke, see a trail in the air. At first I think it must be him, but his hands are behind his back, and I realize, as I see a sporty Mini Cooper, navy blue with a white stripe down the middle and a white hood, zip off, that Farrin must have been out here until a few minutes ago. Students may not be allowed to have cars on campus during the school day, but they are allowed to for after-school activities and special events, and Farrin's car is, of course, that zippy Mini Cooper.

"Farrin drove me over tonight," Jack says, as if I just asked, which, obviously, I didn't. "But she had somewhere else to go afterward. I'm just waiting for my dad."

"Oh."

Well, aren't I the witty conversationalist?

Jack looks at me, kind of smiles, I think.

"So"—he clears his throat—"what kind of name is

D'Arc? I mean, it sounds so romantic." He coughs again. "So tragic. Is it French? It sounds so . . . guillotine."

This is the first time Jack has really said anything to me, and I am so surprised that he is even talking to me at all, after the ass I made out of myself inside, that I answer truthfully without even thinking about it.

"No," I say. "It's a made-up name."

He digests this for a moment, then nods seriously.

"That was a real hard time you had back there," he says, indicating the gym with a nod of his head.

"Yeah, well," I say, "I guess there are worse things in life." *Like saying dumb-ass things to the most beautiful guy in the world,* I think, wanting to hit myself on the head.

"You took it real well," he says.

It is the strangest thing, but I get the feeling he is trying to tell me that he approves of me somehow.

Even in the dark, I see him blush a bit, like he has been caught out at something.

"Well, I think I'll wait for my dad inside," he says, opening the door to go back into the field house, his voice turning gruff now. "Good night."

"Good night," I say back softly to the closed door.

When basketball tryouts formally end at nine o'clock, Mohammed is there promptly to pick me up. When he dropped me off before, he asked when I'd be done and

I told him. Whenever Helena isn't between us, he is always on time. Sometimes he's so on time when I get to tell him myself when I'll need him that I wonder if he just pushes other customers out of the cab or just drops them in the middle of whatever street they're driving on at the time. Sometimes I picture Mohammed saying cheerily to some man in a business suit who's maybe on his way to the airport, *So sorry, Mr. Businessman, but I must leave you here. It is time to go pick up Miss Ren. Just walk another fifty miles east and you should be all right.* The thought makes me smile.

"So," he asks now eagerly, holding the door open for me, "how did it go?"

"Yea, Panthers," I say halfheartedly.

He must see my expression because his own smile now fades.

"You did not get the ball in the cup?" he says.

"No," I say. "So now it looks like I have to be a cheerleader instead."

But once I'm safe in the dark of the back of the cab, I smile, remembering that even if I have made a total ass out of myself tonight, even if T'Keyah thinks I'm such an uncoordinated jerk that she never wants to be my friend, even if I have to do splits on Farrin's say-so for the rest of my life, at least one good thing has happened.

Jack Nicholas has talked to me for the first time.

From: Shannongirl@yaahoo.com
To: RenD@aaol.com

Oh, R!

I cannot believe that your dad won't let you come to Sheila's party—that sucks! What is <u>wrong</u> with him? So he doesn't want to come into the city with you, so he says going into the city right now makes him miss your mom too much—so what? Why can't he just let you come in by yourself? It's not like, half the time when you lived here all those years, you weren't getting around by yourself, taking a taxi or the subway or whatever. But <u>nooo</u>. Now he's got to get all overprotective and tell you that you can't take the train in by yourself, that he'd be too worried about you all night? This sucks, Ren, it just sucks. Oh, well. Guess I'll just have to have a good enough time for both of us.

Luv,
S

Every school has a Joseph Jones.

Okay, maybe they don't all have someone whose exact name is Joseph Jones. But, believe me, every school has one.

Joseph Jones is the cool teacher. Joseph Jones is the teacher who understands you, probably because he's young himself, not even old enough to be your father. Joseph Jones is hated by the rest of the staff, except for the school secretary, a grandmother who flirts with him mercilessly; and, okay, maybe a few of the female teachers do have crushes on him, even the married ones. The rest of the staff, even the ones with crushes, resent and are suspicious of his ability to connect so effortlessly with his students. They resent the sex appeal he manages to exude while wearing faded jeans and a tweed jacket. They resent that he has all his hair and that the hair in question is thick and blond, like maybe he might be the next Brad Pitt if he weren't already committed to instilling a love of literature in the minds and hearts of his young charges. They resent the fact that Joseph Jones encourages those young charges to call him by his first name, somehow managing to earn more respect rather than losing it by his insistence that no one ever address him as "Mister." In this instance, Joseph Jones is my English teacher. He wants us to call him Jo-Jo. I think I am in love.

I am not alone.

Every girl in every one of Jo-Jo's classes thinks she is in love. Probably the most in love is Farrin, who has a tendency to sit with her heels propped on the metal sidebars of her desk, bare legs spread under the short skirt of her school uniform. If Jo-Jo ever drops his chalk, he will see London, he will see France, he will see Farrin's underpants.

The boys seem a little more suspicious of Jo-Jo, who, like me, is new to the school. I wonder why at first: Maybe it is a testosterone thing? Then I realize: Of *course* it is a testosterone thing! Before Jo-Jo came along, they had no competition among the staff, meaning that Dr. Coleson, Mr. Schmidt, Mr. Davies, and Ron—the headmaster, chemistry teacher, American history teacher, and janitor, respectively—are no competition. Nor is Mr. Welch, although I have yet to figure out what he does other than monitor homeroom. Up until now the boys of Waylord have had the girls of Waylord pretty much to themselves. But now there is a new hombre in town, packing heat. There is a new man for the girls to get all hormonal about. Girls are dropping at his feet like gadflies, and even Farrin Farraway is spreading her legs for the new Union soldier.

The bell rings, and we are all filing out when I hear Jo-Jo call, "Ren? Can you stay behind for a minute? I'll give you a late note for your next class."

I can't believe this. What have I done? It is only the first week of school and I am already in trouble for something. As I wait for everyone else to file out, my notebook clutched to my chest as I stand before Jo-Jo, I think back over the last fifty minutes, trying to figure out what I have done wrong this time. It is not, after all, like the time at Simmons when Shannon and I smuggled a case of my parents' wine into the science fair, getting my whole class slightly drunk, drunk enough for Missy Howell to almost blow up the gym when she lit up her volcano with a butane lighter rather than merely explaining how it was supposed to work. What have I done wrong now? When Jo-Jo spoke of the importance of Sir Arthur Conan Doyle, did I not seem sufficiently interested? Did I—gasp!—yawn?

"Please," Jo-Jo says when everyone is gone, indicating a chair right in front of his desk, "sit."

I obey, while he himself perches on the edge of his desk.

"Look, Ren," he says, "I know how hard this must be for you, coming to a new school after what your family suffered last summer."

I cannot believe this. He is the first teacher at Waylord to refer, even indirectly, to my mother. Even Dr. Coleson did not mention her at my entrance interview. He merely said something vague like, "Change is tough and only the tough adapt well to change." Then he bent his bald head close to mine, looked me straight in the eyes. "How about you? Are you *tough*, Lauren D'Arc?" I looked straight back at him, thinking all the while, *What kind of jack-off thinks a teenage girl should be "tough" about losing her mother just because her mother is a research-addicted writer?* Then I said, "My name is Ren. If you call me Lauren again, I'll kick you in the shins. Is that tough enough for you?" It seemed to be.

"It's okay," I say now, uncomfortable at the idea of Jo-Jo feeling sorry for me. "Worse things have happened to people."

"Hey," he says, "you don't have to put on a front with me. I'm on your side. I just hope you realize that, and I just want you to know that if you need anything while you're here at Waylord, anything at all, if you just want to talk to someone, I'm always here for you, my door is always open."

It is hard to know what to say to this. Since my mother's death, no one's door has always been open to me, not even my father's. Right after she died, he tried to talk to me, but then I guess he could see how hard it was for me to talk to him about her, and I could see how hard it was for him to talk to me about her, and I guess we both just stopped talking. Except for discussing practical details—like where we were going to live and who was and who wasn't going to learn to drive—we converse as if nothing has happened. It's like we're each locked in our own separate worlds, like each of us is trapped inside one of those colorful, shimmery bubbles you blow with a wand when you are really small, able to see each other but not really hear each other.

I want to tell Jo-Jo that I am grateful for the concern in his gray eyes, but there are tears forming behind my own eyes. It probably doesn't help matters any that he looks so cute there, perched on the edge of his desk, the well-defined muscles in his upper arms hinted at as he leans forward, hands loosely resting on his bent knee.

"Thanks," I say roughly, rising to my feet. "I'll keep it in mind."

"You know," he says, "we're really both in the same boat here. You're new, I'm new. I'm your friend here," he says. "Don't ever forget that."

"Yeah, well," I say, "thanks again."

I close the door to Jo-Jo's classroom and finally let the tears come, knowing I will be alone in the hall, since everyone else should be in next period by now.

"Hey, what did he do to you?" I hear a voice say.

Startled, I look up to see Jack Nicholas standing there.

"What?" I say dumbly, not understanding. "What are you doing here?"

"Waiting for you," he says. "I got worried when Jones held you back after class. I wanted to make sure you were okay." He nods his head toward the door angrily, as if the door is Jo-Jo. "What did he say to you?"

"Nothing," I say.

"Then why are you crying?"

I just can't tell him. I can't say the words out loud— that sometimes I miss my mom so much, I can't stand it. Usually, I try not to let myself think about it. But Jo-Jo caused the feelings to leap out of me, and right now the sadness is like a monster I can't control. I know if I tell Jack the truth, I will totally lose it, right here in one of the hallways at Waylord.

"No reason," I finally mumble. "Must just be girl hormones or something."

"Fine," he says, something closing down in his eyes, "keep it to yourself if you want to."

"Jack," I call as he starts to walk away, putting a hand on his arm without thinking about it.

He turns, and now his eyes are softer again. "Hey," he says. "Anytime you decide you're ready to talk . . ."

From: Shannongirl@yaahoo.com
To: RenD@aaol.com

You will <u>not</u> believe what happened at Sheila Wentworth's party! Sheila and—hold on to your chair, now!—<u>Todd</u> hooked up! Can you <u>believe</u> it??? Your body's practically not even <u>cold</u> yet, and already he's moved on to greener meadows or sunnier pastures or whatever you call it. Hey, listen, I wanted to stick up for you. I was all ready to go over and split them up like I was a yardstick between their bodies and tell them <u>exactly</u> what I think of them. But then you'll never guess what else happened! You know how I've been wanting to hook up with Rick, like, <u>for-e-ver</u>—you know Rick, Sheila's older brother, the one in college?—and just as I got up to Todd and Sheila, Rick intercepted me, and, yeah, well, um … <u>yum</u>. So, anyway, you know, I'm sorry, but it's not like you were still thinking you and Todd were going to work out. I mean, you guys are totally broken up, right?

Write soon!
S

From: FDA
To: SexGurl

Okay, I understand your reluctance to send photos over the Internet. I share that reluctance. But how about giving me a little bit more to go on here. For example, if I conducted a formal and thorough exploration, would I discover you're a natural blond or unnatural? Whatever the case, they do say that the journey is the thing. . . .

It's been so long since I've been out on a date. My last real date was with Todd Haynes in Manhattan, the guy I almost had sex with for the first time, meaning for the first time ever and not just with him. We were going to do it to celebrate going back to school in September, because we figured that would give us at least one reason to look forward to going back to school, but then my mother died and my dad decided to move us to Connecticut. I thought we'd keep going out, but Todd said the train ride was too long. And then I said I didn't want to have sex with someone for the first time ever, in my life and not just with that person, if that person thought an hour and twenty minutes spent on a train was just too long to keep on seeing me.

So that was that.

Only now that Shannon tells me Todd has hooked up with Sheila, I am upset. I thought I was over him, but I guess in my mind I must have been thinking that things would eventually work out for us, that he'd come to his senses and realize that an hour and twenty minutes on the train really *isn't* too long, not if you really love someone. "Really love"—that's what I once thought Todd felt for me, that's what I once thought I felt for him.

But now it seems that it was never really like that at all, and Shannon is so caught up in Rick—she keeps e-mailing about him, like she wants me to ask her more about him like a best friend should, which, of course, I do—that I can't talk to her about any of this, and I wish Mom were here so I *could* talk to her about all of this.

Except now I don't have time to think about any of that because Waylord is taking up all my time and mind.

There are so many new things to get used to at Waylord, so many things done differently than where I come from. Take, as just one for instance, something called The Mentor Program.

Older kids are hooked up with younger kids, and each older kid is expected to take the younger kid under his or her wing for the entire year, helping the younger kid academically or socially or really with just anything the younger kid needs help with. The school waits until a few weeks into the fall semester before matching kids up, to give the faculty advisers time to figure out who will work best with whom.

Can you tell my parents are/were authors? I may not always know dick, but I do know my "who" from my "whom."

On a Tuesday, during homeroom, I'm given an envelope with my assignment in it. I slit it open, thinking, *I'm the new one here. Shouldn't I be getting a mentor instead of the other way around?* Sometimes Waylord seems way backward.

The letter says that one Wednesday a month I'll be excused from after-school sports practice to go mentor my mentee. Then it gives the name of my mentee: *Mandy Nicholas.*

Hmm . . . Nicholas, Nicholas, Nicholas . . . Now, where have I heard that last name before?

Well, of course it's Jack's little sister, the girl who looks so much like him, with auburn hair and big brown eyes, and who sits at the back of the bus across the aisle from him and Farrin.

Or is that supposed to be "Farrin and him"?

Whatever.

But on Wednesday it's me sitting at the back of the bus with her, because I'm now her mentor, and, of course, Jack's still at school at basketball practice.

Up close Mandy's eyes are so big, her hair so perfect, she looks like one of those sweet American Girl dolls. But when she talks . . .

"What street do you live on?" she demands. "And what kind of name is Ren, anyway?"

I answer her first question. To her second, I say, "It's a nickname. It's short for Lauren."

"Huh," she snorts, "I can see why you'd abbreviate it."

Hey, I want to say, *Mandy is no great shakes either*, but I'm supposed to be the mentor here, mature and wise, so I keep silent. Maybe she'll think I'm Buddha and start offering me sacrifices. A few sacrifices could be good. Maybe she could start with Farrin?

Bump, bump, bump, the bus bumps along.

"So," she says, "I guess if you live on *that* street, you must be one of the rich bitches in school."

"Well, I wouldn't exactly put it like that."

"But you're the one whose parents are writers, right?"

"Were."

"They got fired?" she sneers.

How does someone so young get so good at sneering? Maybe she's not really younger than Jack. Maybe she's older than Jack, but she's a midget and no one at Waylord realizes this, and Jack's parents, who really should know if their daughter is younger or older than their son, somehow forgot.

"Well, no," I say. "My dad still does it. But my mom died. That's why she doesn't write anymore."

I don't tell her I still write to my mom. It is, quite

frankly, none of her business. Besides, no one knows about my letters to my mom.

"Oh." Mandy looks slightly embarrassed, but only just slightly. "But your dad, he's loaded like R. L. Stine, right?"

"Well, no. I mean, he does okay, but no one's as loaded as R. L. Stine. Except maybe J. K. Rowling."

"But you live on that expensive street, so even if you're not that rich, you're still pretty rich, right?"

Is she a real estate agent? Is she hoping to sell my house?

"I guess," I answer. "I never really thought about it."

"Clearly," she sniffs. "Why do you take the bus? Don't you have your own Rolls-Royce? Or does your *chauffeur* take you around?"

"I don't drive," I say. "I, um, take cabs. How old did you say you were again?"

"I didn't."

"Oh."

"I'm eight, okay? I'm eight, and I'm in third grade with a lot of rich bitches like you. There. Are you satisfied?"

"Not really," I mutter, but my words get lost in the exhaust sounds of the bus as it strains its way up a long, winding hill.

"Almost there," Mandy announces, her small body

thrown backward by the jerking motions of the bus. "Now you're going to see *our* palace."

Okay, so it's not a palace. Instead, it's a beige condo. At least it's a townhouse. But why do they always have to paint condos beige? Don't they realize beige is just so *beige*? It's a depressing color. It even sounds depressing. I mean, if you were going to pick a color to describe your personality, would anyone in the world ever pick *beige*? You might pick chocolate or you might pick caramel or you might even pick tan, if you wanted to work strictly within the brown family of the color spectrum, but I seriously hope you'd never pick beige. Come to think of it, it's like those orange prison jumpsuits you always see now, orange being just about the worst color in the world, right up there tied with beige. I mean, has anyone bothered to stop and give any thought to the fact that there'd be a lot fewer repeat offenders if their minds weren't totally scrambled in the first place by being forced to wear orange every day?

"It's better inside," Mandy says, putting the key in the lock and saving me from exploding my own head with all of my complex thought processes. "At least inside it's not beige."

Hey, maybe this kid is cool after all.

And it is less depressing inside. Even if none of the

furniture is anything I'd ever pick out, the overstuffed pieces in the living room—which is, like, right there as soon as you walk through the door—look comfortable enough. So maybe the room is a little small, but there's a fireplace and a TV, and the dining room, which you can see from the front door, looks, well, cozy.

"Shoes," Mandy growls at me, pointing.

I look down at my feet. "Yes. They are."

"Off," she commands, pointing to a wooden shoe rack I hadn't noticed right in the entryway.

Jeez, I think, slipping out of my Steve Maddens. I can remember, growing up, when you'd go to visit someone and all that was expected of you was wiping your soles on the welcome mat before walking into a house. Now almost everyone makes you take off your shoes. What is up with that? It doesn't make me feel welcome. It makes me feel awkward. It makes me feel as though I'm living my entire life inside a Japanese restaurant . . . in Japan!

What's next? Lounging kimonos? Moments of silent meditation?

"Amanda, honey, is that you?" A woman walks through a doorway just to the right of the dining room. I'm thinking it must be the kitchen, since she's wiping her hands on an apron. God, I didn't know anyone other than maids still wore aprons anymore.

And this is clearly Jack and Amanda's mother; I can tell by the hair and eyes. Suddenly, my nose is hit by some pretty great smells: meat, vegetables, maybe something apple-cinnamony in there. Okay, so maybe it's not like Zabar's or Dean & DeLuca, but it still smells good. It smells like a mom made it.

Upstairs, Mandy's room is surprising and not. It's surprising that an eight-year-old girl should have a room totally devoid of pink and purple, the color scheme being predominately black and silver and white. It's surprising that an eight-year-old girl should have a room totally devoid of dolls and stuffed animals, instead filled with bookcases containing books far beyond her years, the white desk nearly covered with a giant computer, the screen saver of which looks suspiciously like a giant hex sign. But none of it is surprising because the eight-year-old in question is Amanda. I'm only surprised that her bed is a real bed and that she doesn't sleep on a plywood board like a vampire or something.

"So what are you going to ment me about?" she demands, after she changes out of her uniform. "My mentor last year was cooler than you. *She* always smelled like pot."

I raise my eyebrows. "You know what pot smells like?"

"Maybe it was cigarettes. Does it matter? It was definitely something *smoky*."

"Smoke is bad for your lungs," I say.

"Who are you, the surgeon general?"

God, Mandy is nothing like her brother. Jack is so nice, Jack is so real, while Mandy is just *so* so so so . . . *Mandy*. And not only is she just *so* so so so Mandy, the girl is a Bratz doll!

"Maybe you should just tell me what you'd like me to, um, ment you about."

"Well, you could do my math homework for me."

"I'm not going to *do* your math homework for you!"

"I mean, you could help me with it."

Oh, crap. Math.

But then, I think, how hard could third-grade math be?

"Sure," I say, "why not?" At least, I figure, it'll give me something to distract her from what was undoubtedly a forthcoming attack on how my people have exploited the masses.

See? Sociology, I'm great at. Math, not so much.

She opens up a binder to a work sheet, and I look at it, growing more puzzled the longer I look. What can I say? It's all math to me.

Just then Mandy's mother calls up the stairs. Saved by the bell. "Amanda! Come set the table for dinner!"

"Bitch," Mandy mutters under her breath.

"Listen." I point toward the door, where the sound of Mrs. Nicholas's voice just came through loud and clear. "Your mother's voice. You get to hear it every day, even if sometimes it annoys you. But guess what? My mother's dead. I don't get to hear her voice anymore. I'll never hear it ever again. And all the . . . all the . . . all the cabdrivers and chauffeurs in the world won't ever change that."

It's not that I'm trying to lay a guilt trip at her feet or make her feel sorry for me, I swear, but doesn't she realize how much she has?

"A-man-DUH!"

Well, I didn't put that "duh" there.

"Coming!" we again shout in unison.

In the hall I notice there are only two other doors up here, both open. One is obviously a bathroom—I mean, there *is* a toilet in it and everything—while the other is a bedroom with a double bed that looks very parenty.

"Um," I say, "where does Jack sleep?" Not that I'm really curious or anything. You know. About where Jack *sleeps*.

"In the basement."

Poor Jack! Doesn't it get cold down there? And aren't there, like, spiders?

We go to set the table and find Mr. Nicholas already sitting there. I guess he got home from work while we were upstairs and we didn't hear the door; just having too much fun, I guess. Mr. Nicholas, unlike Mrs. Nicholas, does not look at all like Jack. That's okay, though. There's something very comforting about his almost bald head, his gray eyes, and his uncoolly big belly. In a way, he kind of looks like a TV dad.

"Friend of Jack's?" He nods his beer bottle at me.

"Amanda's mentor," Mrs. Nicholas says.

"Ah," says Mr. Nicholas. At least he doesn't waste a lot of time on foolish chatter.

We finish setting the table, and I'm just getting ready to call for a cab—I mean, I've mented long enough for one day, haven't I?—when Mrs. Nicholas invites me to eat with them.

"Really?" I say.

"Any mentor of Amanda's . . . ," she says.

"Thanks."

She asks if I want to use the phone, call home and let them know where I am.

I think of how out of it Dad's been since Mom died. He probably won't even notice I'm not there.

"That's okay," I say. "No need."

But I do ask if I can use the downstairs bathroom to wash my hands.

Of course, I don't really need to wash my hands. I mean, I haven't done anything since I've been here to make them dirty, right? And that experiment with frogs in science lab was hours ago. Surely, those germs are dead by now. Hell, the frog was even dead.

No, I don't need to wash my hands. But I do need to take this opportunity to quietly open the door to the basement—like so; tiptoe down the long flight of stairs, all the while thanking Japanese living for my shoeless feet—like so; turn on the light switch—like so; and, voilà!

Jack's room!

Not that I'm excited to be here or anything.

Jack's room is huge! And it's painted this really peaceful green color, with posters of basketball players on the wall. I wonder if T'Keyah knows Jack Nicholas has a poster of her dad in his basement? There's also what looks like a killer sound system with, like, a gazillion CDs. There's a spare Waylord jacket hanging off the back of a chair in front of a desk with a computer on it. That must be where Jack does his homework!

Obsessed much, Ren?

But so what? This is Jack's room! This is Jack's big double bed!

Surely, no one will notice or mind if I lie down here

just for a second, stare up at the ceiling daydreaming, then let my eyes gently close. . . .

Damn Japanese living that encourages people to take off their shoes when they enter a home! I say "damn Japanese living" because I receive no advance warning before . . .

"Well, would you look at this?" I hear the much-hated voice of Farrin Farraway. "Who are you supposed to be, D'Arc—Goldilocks?"

Snagged.

I'm up and off that bed like a light, all pleasant fantasies fleeing. I blink like you do after you've had your eyes closed for a while, trying to clear your vision, only to see Farrin and Jack in front of me.

Apparently, they had time after sports practice to change into street clothes. Farrin is wearing a really cool little peasant top with a satin, bloodred, tiered skirt that looks like she could have even got it in New York. Next to her, in my Waylord uniform, I feel unsophisticated, childish, *dumb*. So much for uniforms being the great equalizer. As for Jack, in his jeans and yellow T-shirt, he just looks so—

I hear pounding down the stairs, and suddenly, Mandy is right behind them.

"Did you pass out or something?" Jack asks, looking concerned.

"Did you remember to leave a trail of bread crumbs so you can find your way home?" Farrin snickers.

"No," I answer him. "No," I answer her. "We were just about to eat dinner. I guess I just got lost on the way to the washroom."

Mandy gives me an "a likely story" look, but she doesn't say anything. I brush by them.

"Don't want to be late for dinner!" I say brightly, cursing myself for chirping like a bird.

I go upstairs to the small dining room, take the seat Mrs. Nicholas indicates for me at the pine table. There are five place settings.

"Oh, Farrin," Mrs. Nicholas says, as if seeing her for the first time, as she puts a steaming bowl of baked potatoes down on the table. I'm beginning to gather that Mrs. Nicholas does this a lot: looks at people as though seeing them for the first time. "Would you like to stay for dinner too?"

"No, thanks, Mrs. Nicholas," Farrin says. Well, at least she has some small kind of manners. "I was just going to go to McDonald's. We were just dropping off Jack's smelly gym clothes. Come on." She puts her hand on Jack's elbow, gives it a firm tug.

"Jack's going too?" Mrs. Nicholas looks surprised.

"Of course," Farrin says.

From the look on Jack's face, this is news to him, yet he allows himself to be led away.

"I hate that bitch," Mandy says as soon as the door closes behind them.

"Amanda!" Mrs. Nicholas admonishes.

"Well, it's true." Mandy turns to me.

"The kid's got a point," Mr. Nicholas says reasonably, spearing some beef. "It's never made sense to me, what Jack sees in her."

"I'll tell you what Jack sees in her," Mandy says.

Please do, I think.

"He sees money. He sees her Mini Cooper. He sees a way to get around town in her cool car so that no one at Waylord will guess that we've got less than most everyone else."

This is a stunner.

"Jack is . . . shallow?" I say.

"No, of course my brother's not shallow," Mandy says. "What are you—stupid? He's just normal. He's just like everyone else. He wants to fit in."

I guess that makes sense. Sort of.

"Plus," Mandy goes on, "when Farrin is around Jack, she doesn't act the same as she does around everyone else. She's nicer somehow. And even when she's not, it's like Jack doesn't really notice it."

That sounds like the Jack I've been getting to

know—seeing more in people than what's actually there, or maybe even seeing the best in them.

"But she's still a bitch," Mandy says. Then she looks at me thoughtfully. "I'd give anything to get Jack away from her."

I look back at her thoughtfully. *Me too*, I think.

We don't talk about Jack or Farrin anymore. We just continue eating our meal. The food is nothing spectacular, yet somehow, it feels so good. At least it feels like having dinner with a real family, even if one of them is a Bratz doll.

And after dinner and apple pie, they won't even let me call a cab to come get me. Instead, they insist on driving me home.

It is hard to believe that two people who are as different from each other as Farrin and me can have the exact same taste in spiral-bound notebooks. Hers is covered in fake-fur zebra stripes with a hot pink feather trim, and so is mine. They look like giant, almost flat pocket-books, the feathers attached to the handles.

It is those zebra notebooks that finally begin the unraveling of the truth.

I am sitting with the cheerleading squad at lunch. As usual, Farrin is mostly ignoring me, even though today we are seated directly across from each other. As not so usual, Farrin does not seem like her normal self. She is somehow happier, edgier, and less bitchy all at once, as though there is something big on her mind. I think she must be thinking of the first dance of the year—the Sadie Hawkins Dance—which is coming up fairly soon. Is she thinking about asking Jack? He is sitting at the next table, looking at us.

Farrin and I never talk, except for when she yells at

me at cheerleading practice, but now that she is right across from me, I feel like an idiot just sitting here, not saying anything, as though we don't even know each other, as though we don't even know the other person's name.

"Have you decided yet," I blurt, "who you're going to ask to the Sadie Hawkins Dance?"

Inside, I am thinking, *Please don't let it be Jack, please don't let it be Jack, please don't let it be Jack.* Although, who else could it be? She is the most sought-after girl in the school. He is the most sought-after boy. Who else would each go with, if not each other?

She stares at me for a long minute, and then she laughs so hard—the laugh just one huge snort—that some of the chocolate milk she's just sipped from her little carton comes back out her nose.

She covers her nose and mouth with her hand, each fingernail a work of high-priced manicurist art, for once embarrassed.

Then she glares at me, like it's all my fault she can't control her drinking.

"*Why,*" she says, leaning across the table, each word coming at me like a silk bullet, "would *I* want to go to some *stupid kiddie dance*?"

Then she gets up from the bench with high-breasted dignity, as though there aren't a couple of chocolate milk stains now decorating the front of her pristine white blouse, unbuttoned low enough to show off some serious cleavage, picks up her notebook, tosses it on her tray, grabs the tray, and stalks off.

I think perhaps Farrin is protesting too much? Maybe she is acting like she would never want to go to the dance when she knows that, in reality, she will be going with the guy I most want to go with and that it will be more of a blow to me if I find this news out at the last minute, like, say, when I walk into the dance, than if I find it out right this minute and therefore have plenty of time to mentally adjust?

I watch her stalk off.

Farrin is so dramatic that if she didn't annoy me so much and if I liked girls in that way, I would fall in love with her.

But, of course, the zebra notebook she grabs isn't her notebook. It's mine. And I now have hers, which I'm going to find out just as soon as I open it to get out my paper for English class.

It is tough to keep my mind on English when what I am really thinking is this: *If Farrin isn't going to ask Jack to the Sadie Hawkins Dance, then maybe I can ask him? Because maybe I was giving her too much credit before when I was second-guessing her motives and, in actuality, she really isn't interested in the dance?*

But I have always hated getting up in front of a class to read a paper, hate the idea of everyone staring at me, so I arrive early for Jo-Jo's class, hoping to spend the extra ten minutes reading over my essay on Fitzgerald one last time. I have picked Fitzgerald because, from everything Jo-Jo's said about him, I know how much Jo-Jo likes him, and, well, I can be a bit of a suck-up.

I sit at my desk in the quiet room, open up the zebra notebook expecting to find "*The Great Gatsby:* A Good Reason for Not Swimming Alone." Instead, I find:

From: FDA
To: SexGurl

Hey, I saw you talking to the others in the chat room, and I really like your style. You can tell so much about a woman from the way she writes.
So, tell me, really, how old are you?

Immediately, I realize what has happened: Farrin has taken my notebook and I have hers. But that makes Farrin . . . SexGurl???

I study the sheet in front of me. It's basic copy paper, but the sheet is worn, as though someone has read it many times, like a well-loved love letter. But this is like no love letter I've ever seen before, not that I've seen all that many of them, except maybe in books. Oh, no. At the top of the sheet there's a large graphic—Sex World—and I realize I'm looking at a printout of a private exchange from a website.

This top sheet is dated several weeks ago, and there are at least thirty more pages underneath it. I know it's wrong to read someone else's mail, but I can't help myself. What is Farrin doing on one of those icky sites? Everyone knows that only perverts hang out there. If a girl—or "gurl"—tries to hook herself up with some guy she meets at one of those places, a girl/gurl can get herself killed!

I finally get to the last printout, dated just the night before.

From: FDA
To: SexGurl

Honey, I'm getting really desperate here. I don't know how much more of this I can stand. Are you going to agree to meet me or aren't you? You know you want to as badly as I do. Don't pretend otherwise. I wouldn't want to have to move on to someone else—who could ever be as perfect for

me as you?—but I have to tell you, if I don't see
you in and then out of that school uniform soon,
I think I'm going to have to do something drastic.
Of course, it's your call. I just hope you'll make
the right one.

What a creep! What a manipulative jack-off! Why
would Farrin want to be with someone like this in the
first place? Of course, she will write back to him and
tell him to move on to someone else, that she's not
really interested in any guy who is obviously a child
molester.

But then I think back on the letters I've just read.
Even though the printouts are only of what FDA has
written to SexGurl, there is an undeniable progression
to them, and it is easy to see that whatever SexGurl
has been writing back in between, she has been giving
FDA encouragement. If something doesn't happen to
stop that progression, SexGurl, scared of losing the
attention of FDA, will undoubtedly agree to meet with
FDA in some out-of-the-way place, neglecting to tell
anyone where she's going, and wind up getting her
pretty little throat slit in the process. Or worse.

Someone will have to stop this before it happens.

But how?

I see the shadow across my desk before I hear

the voice. Instinctively, I snap my notebook—Farrin's notebook—shut on the incriminating evidence.

"So, Ren," says Jo-Jo, his thick hair looking even more golden from the sunshine streaming through the window behind him, creating a kind of halo effect, "are you ready to wow the class with your views on F. Scott Fitzgerald?"

I know my dad would say it is trite, but I am like a goddamned deer in the goddamned headlights, because of course I don't have my *Gatsby* paper to read, because it's in the notebook that's in Farrin's hands as she enters the room, glaring at me. And since I don't want her to know I've read her private papers, I can't tell her we need to switch notebooks, because then she'd know I've opened hers, and I can't let her even suspect that I've opened her notebook, so I tell Jo-Jo that I'm going to give my report without notes, which totally impresses him, but when I stand up in front of the class, I can't remember a single fucking thing about F. Scott Fitzgerald or his stupid book, so my mind seizes instead on another of Jo-Jo's three favorite authors, Jane Austen—just yesterday Dylan Zimmerman, another suck-up if I ever met one, read his paper on Jo-Jo's other favorite writer, Sir Arthur Conan Doyle—and I mumble for ten minutes about how if Jane Austen were writing today, the male-dominated literary establishment would brand her books as "chick lit."

What can I say? It's something I heard my mother say repeatedly before she died, and like everything else Mom said repeatedly—things like "Don't hang out in Internet chat rooms where the focus is sex, because that's a good way to wind up dead"—it's probably true.

Anyway, Jo-Jo is impressed at least.

But there is one person who is definitely not impressed: Farrin. When she goes to open her own notebook, which is really my notebook, to give her paper on the author of the Gossip Girl series of books of all things, she discovers my Fitzgerald paper on top instead.

Gee, I think, *I hope she's too busy to notice that on the inside flap of my notebook I've written Jack Nicholas's name in florid handwriting with a tiny heart dotting the* i.

Thankfully, she is too busy to notice, because she's too busy being miffed at me.

"Did you lose something, D'Arc?" She waves my paper in the air. If a waved paper can taunt, that's what's happening. Then she realizes what you and I have known all along: If she has my notebook, then I must have hers.

She rises from her chair, stands in front of my desk

menacingly, points to the notebook on the table.

"You didn't read anything in there, did you, D'Arc?" she demands.

"Of course not," I lie first. Then I play dumb: "But what are you doing with my Gatsby paper? And why would it matter if I read anything in my own notebook?"

"Because it's not your notebook," she says, gritting her teeth as she snatches hers up, replacing it with mine. "It's mine."

Five minutes later, halfway through listening to her read from her paper, "Gossip Girls: It's Not Just About Shoes and Makeup Anymore," it occurs to me: I cannot believe I am going to have to find a way to save this bitch from a fate that would probably be worse than death.

From: FDA
To: SexGurl

Tell me something about yourself that supposedly only I know, so I can be sure it's you. Tell me about that tattoo again. Describe it for me, what it looks like, where it's located. . . .

By the time I get home from school, I know exactly what I am going to do.

Or at least I think I do.

I am going to impersonate Farrin so that I can trap this creep.

But first I have to become SexGurl.

I fly off the bus, fly up the stairs to my room, stopping only long enough to grab a giant cupcake with chocolate icing from Mrs. Johnson in the kitchen and to pop in my dad's study, kiss him on the head as he works on his computer. He always works so hard.

When we first moved here, perhaps not wanting me to be depressed about the move, not to mention depressed about everything else, my dad did his best to re-create my bedroom from New York City right here in Danbury, Connecticut. In fact, even though he got mostly new furniture for the house, especially for his own bedroom, he pretty much moved my whole room from New York intact. So I still have the same glossy white Cape Cod bed I grew up with, the same matching end tables and desk. I've got the same fantasy fairy canopy netting hanging down from the ceiling around it—hey, fairies are cool no matter how old you get—and I've even got the same multicolored hooked rug my mom made one summer between working on books. If you don't know it's there, you don't even notice the shadow stain from the Christmas I had the flu and threw up all over the rug, the Christmas my mother stayed up with me all night, telling me stories, because even though I was so sick, I just couldn't sleep. Dad even went so far as to match the paint on the walls, so now my new walls are close to, if not an exact copy of, the peachy pink I had in the city. But, of course, this is not the city. I mean, it is a city, but it is not *the* city. The people here aren't the same, the sounds aren't the same—it's too damn quiet—and especially what I see when I look out the window is not the same.

I mean, who needs so much damn grass and so many trees?

I put the giant chocolate cupcake on the desk next to my computer, but not before taking a big lick out of the icing—yum!—and boot up my computer, heading straight for Sex World, which suddenly sounds to me like Disney World but without the mouse.

The site claims that you have to be over eighteen to post on it, but it's surprisingly easy to lie on a computer, easy to change the year of my birth. Who is there to check my ID?

But once I'm on, I encounter a problem right away, because the dialog box demands that I select a screen name and I want to be "SexGurl." But, of course, "SexGurl" is already taken. I try "Sex-Gurl," but the dialog box refuses it, saying screen names have to be composed solely of letters and/or numbers and must contain no other punctuation marks. So I finally settle on "SexGurl1." After all, FDA has to be able to recognize me or this won't work.

Now that I have an acceptable name, the site asks me if I want to further detail my profile—eye color? height? weight? interests? I ignore all those optional fields, anxious to get through all these preliminaries . . . until I see a question about geography: Do I want to limit my attendance in chat rooms to those frequented by people in my own geographical region? *Hmm*, I think. Yes, I guess I do. I mean, FDA is pushing for a personal meeting with SexGurl, right? So he probably lives somewhere around here. But how far away? How far away will a pervert travel to hook up with a young private school girl in uniform? In any case, it occurs to me that Farrin and FDA must have found their way to each other via this screen option, so I quickly type in my zip code. I could have picked something more general, like the state as a whole or the county, but that could mean an awfully expensive cab ride. . . .

And then another thing occurs to me: Before I hook up with him, I have to disable her, meaning Farrin. Because, surely, this won't work if she keeps communicating with him. For one thing, maybe she'd agree to meet him before I can set something up, before I can get my sting in gear. For another, he might get suspicious if suddenly he's getting messages from two of us, both saying similar things.

So I commit the ultimate betrayal. I pretend to be Farrin's parents.

True, I could just as easily do that with FDA, pretend to be Farrin's parents and warn him to get away from our daughter. But that would solve the problem of FDA only in the short term. Sure, Farrin would be free of him, but he'd still be free to pursue other teenage girls.

So before writing my first private chat message to FDA, I write to Sex World:

Dear Sex World,
   You may not be aware of this fact, and I'm sure your website is totally innocent of any wrongdoing, but my daughter, Farrin Farraway, who posts on your site under the odious name "SexGurl," is a mere sixteen years old

and not the eighteen required by law to participate in your, um, shall we say, fun and games. I would hate to have to sue the fucking crap out of you, you fucking cocksuckers, but if you don't block her from posting on your site immediately and permanently, I will bring all the powers that Farraway, Fitzgerald, and Austen, Attorneys at Law, has to bear right down on your pedophilic asses.

Cordially,

Farley Farraway

Ha! Who ever said I couldn't write? And I would bet almost anything that Sex World will never look into the authenticity of Farley Farraway, that they'll never learn that Farrin's real father works on Wall Street and knows more about trades than trials.

Feeling an excitement in the pit of my stomach, I take another big lick of the frosting on top of my cupcake, take an even bigger breath, and write my first letter to FDA as SexGurl1.

Almost immediately, he writes back, expresses surprise at the change in SexGurl's screen name, wants to know if it's still the same girl now that there's that additional "1." He wants proof that I am her.

Probably the only advantage of taking off your clothes with a bunch of girls in a cold locker room is that even though there's the downside of them getting to see you in your bra and panties, you get to see them as well. This means that I've seen Farrin bend over, with only her Victoria's Secret black thong on, to take off her gym socks, her back to me, the floss line of that black thong separating two perfectly cellulite-free globes of fake-tan flesh. As a result, I can answer FDA's question with confidence.

From: SexGurl1
To: FDA

On my upper right, um, buttock, there's a single red rose with crossed sabers over it.

Again, almost immediately, he writes back.

From: FDA
To: SexGurl1

"Buttock"? Isn't that word a little . . . delicate? If I recall correctly, the first time you told me about it, you referred to it as "the apple of your ass." What gives? Are you turning shy on me all of a sudden? And what gives with the "1"? Is that you there?

Since I'd only seen FDA's messages to Farrin, but not hers to him, I am at a real disadvantage here, not knowing what she normally sounds like. But I am already getting the impression that, apparently, she is accustomed to being raunchier than I am.

I need to think quickly here. I don't want to lose him, and if he starts thinking I'm not hot enough, he'll move on to some other girl. And then where will I be? I will have lost my chance to expose him. I close my eyes and pretend I'm Farrin, trying to channel her raunchy spirit. Then I have to remind myself to open them again in time to see what I'm typing so that I don't wind up sending something with "kx.dzh.ivfgzs/" all over it. What can I say? My touch-typing sucks.

From: SexGurl1
To: FDA

Oh, but—*purr*—I just thought you might like something a bit . . . different for a change. Don't they say variety is the spice or something like that? And don't forget, one of my attractions is my youth. I just thought maybe you'd find me even . . . sexier if I sounded even younger. I really only did it to please you. But if you don't like . . .

And it is just that easy. Before I know it, FDA is eating out of SexGurl1's young hand.

The afternoon goes on like that, with rapid-fire messages exchanging between us. As I write, as I read, I feel a strange sensation inside me. It takes me a while before I recognize it for what it is: It is excitement. And for the first time I can understand why Farrin is doing this. It is exciting, thrilling, it is totally flattering to have this man, whoever he is, hanging on my every word, picking my words apart as if each one matters, as if *I* matter. It is the most exciting thing to happen to me since moving to Danbury. It is a feeling of power like I've never known. I am in total control of another human being who appears to be totally attracted to me, without ever having met me, without ever having seen me.

But then, of course, I lose control of the situation.

From: FDA
To: SexGurl1

So. Come on, now. You've used delaying tactics long enough. Are you going to finally agree to meet me? Or are you going to say that you've just been stringing me along and that it's time for me to move on?

This is my last chance. I can tell him I don't think it's a good idea. I can chicken out. But then what will happen to the next girl he tries this on? Maybe she won't be so lucky. Maybe she'll agree to meet him somewhere, and then he'll rape her, or even if he doesn't have to rape her, maybe he'll slice and dice her body into little bits afterward?

I just can't take that chance. I still haven't worked out the how, as in: How will I catch him once I catch him? Meaning, he's a man, I'll be alone with him, and I'm not very big. Will I call the police and have them lie in wait? Will I *really* arrange a sting operation? I just don't know yet. But I do know that I need to act quickly or I'll risk losing his attention.

Like I'm in a dream, I watch my own hands as I slowly type:

From: SexGurl1
To: FDA

Yes. I'll meet you. All you have to do is tell me where and when. Wherever it is, whenever it is, I'll be there. I'll come to you.

All afternoon it's seemed that no sooner do I send a message than I receive one in return. But this time it takes forever, the clock on the wall ticking away, and I begin to wonder if maybe *he's* the one who's going to chicken out. Maybe he's all talk and no action and, now that he's got a girl on the hook, he'd rather shut up than put up. Maybe, I think, there will be a reprieve for me.

But there is no reprieve.

From: FDA
To: SexGurl1

You have no idea how happy you've made me. It feels like I've been waiting for this moment forever. Meet me a week from Friday at 8:00 p.m. at the Starshine Motel on Rte. 6. I'll reserve a room— details to follow—so that you can pick up a key if you get there early because you're eager. I'd like it if you were eager. And I promise to be a total gentleman. By the way, how will I recognize you? After all, we've never exchanged pictures, and while that tattoo sounds lovely, I doubt I'll be able to see it right away.

Shit! That's all I can think when I read what he wants. A week from Friday at eight o'clock? But that's the night of the Sadie Hawkins Dance! How can I ask Jack to go with me—not that I've even decided I'm definitely going to do that yet—when I'll be busy trapping this pervert? Shit!

I'm tempted to write FDA back, suggest we make it some other night. But there's such a commanding tone to his last letter, and I've got an uneasy feeling that if I tamper with his itinerary now, maybe he'll back off, decide I'm not worth it.

Half my mind watches Jack recede, getting farther from me than ever, while the other half watches as my fingers type out my own doom.

From: SexGurl1
To: FDA

You'll know me because I'll be the only one with a tiny rose tattoo with crossed swords running through it on my ass. Believe me, you'll see it soon after I arrive, and then you'll know. Friday at 8:00 it is.

After that, there is silence. And even though I have never heard this man's voice, I know what he would tell me: *After all this typing, all these words between us, there is no need for any more talk, because the decision has finally been made.*

For the first time I wonder what "FDA" stands for. It seems so weird. I mean, I've looked around in the public part of the chat room long enough to see the kind of screen names other people use—Big Guy, Little Lolita, The Deflowerer—and it seems strange that this guy would use initials instead of something more suggestive. Perhaps they mean something to him? I think and I think, but the only thing I can think of is the Food and Drug Administration. The Food and Drug Administration is trying to seduce Farrin? No, I realize, that can't be right.

Whatever it stands for, I will find out soon enough, since I'll be meeting FDA in a motel room a week from Friday at eight p.m.

I start wondering what I should wear. It's been so long since I've been out on a date. My last real date was with Todd Haynes in Manhattan, the guy I almost had sex with for the first time, meaning for the first time ever and not just with him. Perhaps I may have mentioned this already?

But somehow, I know that whatever I would wear on a date with Todd Haynes would not be the same thing I would wear to go meet FDA at the Starshine Motel. I get the feeling that, before too much more time has passed, perhaps sometime next week, I will need to call a taxi to take me shopping at the mall.

I cannot believe that my first date in forever will be with a pervert at the Starshine Motel.

Mrs. Johnson calls up the stairs that dinner's ready, and I quickly turn off my computer, wash up, head downstairs. I get to the dining room table—yum, lasagna—only to find my dad not there yet. He really does work too hard.

I go to his office, push the door open, sneak up behind him. I'm just about to lay another kiss on his head when I see him reach for a sheet of paper that's coming out of the copier. I look at the screen to see what he's printing, and I see he's working on his correspondence. He gets a fair amount of fan mail, and, hard worker that he is, he always answers each one personally. Even the whack-jobs.

I watch as he places the sheet to his right, picks up his Montblanc pen, the one I gave him for his last birthday using the AmEx Gold Card he gave me, and I continue watching as he signs that familiar and distinctive signature of his:

FD'A.

I look at it, and I'm thinking of how much I love my dad, how sad I am that he's become so permanently sad, when it hits me: The Sex World dialog box said screen names with punctuation marks are not allowed. And if I remove that tiny little apostrophe from my dad's signature, his name will read *FDA*.

Oh. My. God.

My dad is FDA.

My dad is a sex pervert.

Stunned, I sneak back out of the room. Once I'm away from that desk, away from his computer, I shake my head, like a dog shaking off a surprise bath or a person shaking off a nightmare.

I almost laugh out loud at my own idiocy. Of course my dad isn't FDA. How could he be? It's just not possible.

But then, without wanting to, I remember a few damning facts from what I've read this afternoon.

FDA wrote Farrin: *You can tell so much about a woman from the way she writes.*

This is the kind of thing my dad *always* used to say to my mom.

FDA wrote Farrin: *My most fulfilling fantasies revolve around literary heroines.*

Omigod, that is my dad all over. He always used to tell my mom she was the love of his life, but that if Elizabeth Bennet ever came to life, she could give my mom a run for her money.

What kind of man says those kinds of things to a woman? I'll tell you what kind of man. A literary man, like my dad, who is also . . .

No, I can't think of that.

But then I think: Why did my dad *really* move us

out of the city? Maybe it had nothing to do with wanting a new start for me at all. Maybe he had a *darker* reason. Maybe it had something to do with him doing bad stuff there like he's doing here now.

And now the thought comes back again, only this time I can't stop it:

Oh. My. God.

My dad is FDA.

My dad is a sex pervert.

A week from Friday, I have a date with my own father, the sex pervert, at the Starshine Motel.

You know that saying? The one about rain? Well, let me tell you, it's totally true: When it rains, it *really* rains. And this is a good thing, because it gives me time to distract myself, gives me something to do so that I don't have to do anything right away about my pervy dad. It gives me time to be Hamlet.

Jo-Jo taught us all about Hamlet, in case you don't know all about him yet; all about Hamlet, I mean, not Jo-Jo. Hamlet was this guy in Denmark whose uncle killed Hamlet's father by pouring poison into his ear while he slept so that he—the uncle—could then marry his mother. Hamlet's mother. Who was pretty much in on the whole thing. Then Hamlet spends the next four hours, if you're watching the movie, or days, if you're reading the play, trying to decide what to do, and for the longest time he's not able to *do* anything. To do? To not do? It's a tough dilemma. So that's me now, exactly like Hamlet. Well, except that no one killed my dad and J. K. Rowling did kill my mom. But other than that, really, it's exactly the same.

So it's a good thing that while I'm busy being Hamlet, there are other things going on; specifically, the fact that, not having been invited anywhere in what seems like forever, I'm invited to two parties for the same night.

Count them. Yes, *two*.

First, Kiki Rodriguez asked me if I'd go to a big party she's having this Saturday at her house in Ridgefield; she and T'Keyah live on, like, the same street or something. This is the first really big thing that's happened to me since starting at Waylord. Well, if you don't count meeting Jack and kind of falling for him; meeting Farrin and making it onto the cheerleading team—even though it's no real accomplishment since, like, everyone has to make something at this damn school—and having her always give me a hard time; getting in the middle of some big e-mail sex scandal; and finding out my dad should be shut away somewhere he can't hurt anybody. But this is the first *social* thing that has happened to me, and so of course I say yes.

No sooner is the word "yes" out of my mouth—okay, so maybe it was a few hours later, after I got home from school—than I receive an e-mail from Shannon. Well, actually, first I'd written to her about being asked to Kiki's party. Of course I told her I was going.

From: Shannongirl@yaahoo.com
To: RenD@aaol.com

R,

What shitty timing! I mean, of course I'm <u>glad</u> for you that you're finally going to be getting out and about in that boring little state you somehow got yourself stuck in. But I'm also totally bummed! Because, guess what? <u>I'm</u> having a party Saturday night too! It was a sudden decision—otherwise, you know I would have written to ask you sooner—but I was just about to e-mail to ask you when I got your e-mail saying you're doing something else that night. Bummer! Bummer!! Bummer!!! Oh, well. What's a girl to do? Since you already said yes to this Kiki person, of course you can't now say no to her, so I guess we'll just have to do something, just the two of us, some other time. That's okay. It's probably better this way. So have fun at your party! And don't forget your old friends!

Luv,
S

Shit! Two parties in one night! What would Hamlet do?

Oh, that's right. Hamlet wouldn't do *anything*.

But I had to do *something*, so I wrote to my mom.

Dear Mom,

    I've developed a few, er, problems since the last time we spoke.

1) There's something wrong with Dad. No, no, he's not sick! Well, not like the flu sick. I mean, he hasn't been throwing up on the rug or anything. But there's definitely something really wrong with Dad, but of course I can't tell you about it just yet because I don't want you to worry. I know how you always worry. Just think good thoughts and send them our way, okay? I know you're good at thinking good thoughts.

2) I was invited to TWO parties in one night! This would be okay if they were close together, meaning I could go to one, leave early, then go to the other, arriving late. But the problem is that one is in Ridgefield, CT, and the other is in New York City.

    Oh my gosh, this is amazing! I swear, it's like I can hear you talking to me! You're saying, "Well, you did say yes to Kiki first, so you really should go to her party. Not to mention, it would be good for you to get closer to some of the kids in the Danbury area, now that your school is here and your life _is_ here." BUT, you add, "But Shannon is your oldest friend. Well, at least you've known her a lot longer than you have anyone at Waylord. And if you're really worried about something involving your father, something that's clearly troubling you greatly, don't you owe it to yourself to have an F2F with someone who knows you and your father? Maybe Shannon could help."

God, Mom, I _love_ you! This is the most perfect advice _ever_! (Even though I am kind of surprised to learn you even know what an F2F _is_.)

Talk to you soon! And thanks for everything!

Love,
Ren

And, of course, the advice I imagined my mom giving me *was* the most perfect advice. Well, except for me imagining her saying "F2F"; I don't think Mom ever knew what that meant. But other than that, it was *perfect*! To be honest, I've been dying to write Shannon or call her and tell her what's been going on, but I've been scared to. I mean, seeing as my dad's this big online sex pervert and everything, he's obviously a little more tech-savvy than I previously gave him credit for; he always told me he could barely type books on his computer. What if I e-mailed Shannon about him and my newly tech-savvy dad somehow intercepted it? Of course, if he was *that* tech-savvy, he'd know that the e-mails he used to get from Farrin were no longer coming from her computer but were coming from his own house. But still . . . Did you ever see the movie *When a Stranger Calls*? Well, this is exactly like that—the evil person is right inside my house, only there are no babysitters or small children involved, and no one's dead *yet*—and there's just no way I'm going to risk phone calls or e-mails under those circumstances. I can't leave anything that can be traced. Well, I can't leave anything *else* that can be traced that I haven't left already.

But my mom is right: I owe it to myself to go see Shannon. But I'll surprise her. I won't tell her I'm coming, and I'll get there in the afternoon so I can help her set up. And while I'm helping her set up, we can talk about me me me. Which sounds kind of selfish, but sometimes you have to talk about me me me, and who else in the world is there to talk to about me me me than your best friend in the world?

Of course, Kiki will totally understand, right? I mean, how can she not?

"I totally don't understand," Kiki says when I call her on Saturday morning to tell her I can't come to her party that night.

"I totally don't understand how you can do this to Kiki," T'Keyah says a moment later after Kiki calls and tells her I'm not coming, turning this thing into a conference call.

"We thought you wanted to be our friend, D'Arc," Kiki says.

"Kiki was trying to be nice to you, D'Arc," T'Keyah says, "and this is how you repay her? You punt her for better plans?"

Now they're beginning to sound like Farrin.

Click. T'Keyah hangs up on me.

Click again. There goes Kiki, too.

And here I thought we were all going to be such good friends. I'd even, filled with hope, stored their phone numbers in my home and cell phones, the two of them being the first speed-dial numbers I'd programmed, other than Wheels Instead of Heels, since moving to Danbury.

Rats.

And so begins what will turn out to be the longest night ever. Except that it's still daytime, and pretty early in the day at that.

I would be more upset by this, T'Keyah and Kiki being so mad at me—I mean, I am upset by this, but I would be even *more* upset by this—if I weren't so excited about seeing Shannon. Plus, what kind of great new friends can T'Keyah and Kiki be if they can't understand something as basic as me wanting to go see my oldest and best friend, my best friend I haven't seen in months, when I get to see them every day? Them, I'll see again at school in two days. But if I don't go see Shannon today, who knows when I'll get another chance? Also, I have something important to tell Shannon, something deep and dark that I can tell only her.

The only problem is, I'm so happy at the idea of seeing Shannon again, so *giddy*, it's tough for me to keep the smile off my face, tough to keep myself from flying down the stairs, all joy in a teenage body.

Not even the sight of my dad at the breakfast table can ruin my mood today.

"You're kind of dressed up for a Saturday morning, aren't you?" he asks, briefly looking up from his omelet.

He's sitting in the kitchen, a sunny yellow room that usually gets on my nerves because it's just too cheerful. There's a mess all over the counter. So I know he made the omelet for himself because it is Saturday and Mrs. Johnson, who would never leave a mess, doesn't work on the weekends; plus, when my dad makes omelets, he always burns the edges, and his edges are burnt.

I look down at what I'm wearing: a short white skort from American Eagle Outfitters—which will have to do, because everyone in New York has seen everything in my old wardrobe and this was the best thing I could find at the mall in a pinch—and a tight little aqua tank thingy with an unbuttoned white gauzy blouse over it, plus heels to make me look taller than very short, plus jewelry, plus makeup, which I don't usually wear since moving to Danbury. Why waste the good stuff? If I were still going to Kiki's tonight, I'd wear something more casual, but this is New York City I'm going to—I'm going back to New York City!—and I want to look hot hot hot. Who knows? Maybe Todd'll be at Shannon's party. Maybe I'll win Todd back from Sheila. . . .

Sure, I like Jack now and everything. And, sure, Todd dumped me and doesn't even deserve me back. But what can I say? Hey, I'm a teenager. I'm *conflicted*.

I tell my dad about Shannon's party tonight. I tell

him I've already called Wheels Instead of Heels and that Blue is on her way.

"You're going into the city?" he says, finally looking up from his burnt omelet for more than a second. "You're going into the city, and you didn't even bother to ask me first?" This is the most interest he's shown in talking to me since, well, since Mom died. "I thought I told you not too long ago that I do not want you going to the city."

"It's totally safe," I say. I will *not* let him stop me now. "Blue will take me straight to the train station. I'll take the train in, I'll take a cab to Shannon's, then I'll exactly reverse the process when I come home. What could be easier?"

"I'm still not sure. . . ."

"C'mon, D—" Somehow, I can't bring myself to call him Dad. Not when I know that the *D* that I just let slip out is now indelibly surrounded in my mind with two other letters, which are *F* and *A*, which spell "FDA," which stands for trouble, right here in Danbury city. Hey, do you think there could be a song in there somewhere?

"C'mon," I say, "when we lived in the city, you let me go anywhere I wanted to." Not quite true, but close enough. "And this'll be even safer than that. Before, I used to always take the subway to get around—"

"You took the *subway*?"

"—but now," I steamroll, ignoring him, "I'll be even safer, because it'll be cabs cabs cabs all the way. Well, except for the train part. But even Metro-North is cleaner than it used to be. It must be safer!"

"If your mother were here—"

"She'd say yes," I say emphatically. Who knows this better than me? Don't I write letters to Mom all the time, and doesn't she always sort of answer? Wasn't *she* the one who told me I should go see Shannon? "Mom would most definitely say yes."

"You know," he says, picking up his fork again and spearing a burnt piece of egg, "you're right. Your mother would say yes. So sure, why not? Do you need any extra cash?"

This is the part where, if this were before I read those sex e-mails and not after, I'd throw my arms around my dad's neck and thank him for being so great. Then I'd take the money. I mean, wouldn't you? But this *is* after, and I just can't bring myself to do it.

"No, that's okay," I say, backing up toward the front door as if my dad has the plague, which he kind of does. I wave my gold glitter handbag in the air. "I've still got my AmEx card."

Then I flee.

. . .

Fleeing would be great if it actually got me to where I wanted to go—New York City!—any faster, but as it is, I stand on the curb, waiting waiting waiting, because Blue is late. Did Helena, the dispatcher from hell, *not* give her my message?

But then there Blue is, only forty-five minutes late. When I climb into the back, I notice that the six-foot Amazon's orange-red hair scrapes against the roof of the cab. And feeling scared of her like I always do, I don't dare complain about how upset I am, even though I know I missed the train I wanted to take. Danbury isn't exactly the biggest city in the world, you know, and the train I want stops here only once every couple of hours.

"You look nice, kid," Blue says, eyeing me in her rearview mirror.

"Thanks," I say, feeling weird. Blue has never complimented me before. Maybe it's that I've never looked nice before, but I always assumed it's because Blue herself isn't, well, nice.

"Did you have somewhere special you had to be in the city by a certain time?" Blue asks me in the mirror, cutting a corner one-handed, so sharp and so fast, I get thrown to the other side. Where did all this happy chatter come from? Maybe she should just *drive*?

"Not really," I say. "I just wanted to get there . . . early."

"Well, I'm really sorry about that."

"Helena again?" I hope she hears the sincere sincerity in my voice.

"No." She shakes her head. "My mother. She's got that Alzheimer's thing—you know?—and when she left a message last night saying she was baking, I figured I'd better swing by there today and make sure she didn't burn the place down."

When she talks, Blue always sounds like she could maybe be a Brazilian guy named Pedro, only without the Brazilian accent, but that's neither here nor there. This is no time to be snarky. Blue has a mom! Blue has a sick mom! And Blue even takes care of her!

I don't have much experience with people's moms being sick, though; I only have experience with people's moms getting killed so it's tough to know what to say.

"Is your mom, um, tall," I say, "like you?"

"Nah," Blue says, careening into the train station parking lot, "she's a shrimpo, like you."

Blue is nothing if not full-service, and no sooner does the cab screech to a halt than she's out of her door and opening mine. She's even added a new touch since the last time I drove with her—a black patent-leather cap she puts on, which I think she means to look like a chauffeur's cap but on her looks like she's in the Russian army or maybe a member of Sex World. Or maybe both.

"Army?" I ask, stepping out.

"Nah," she says, "I'm thinking of going pro." She closes my door and opens her own. "Listen, kid, I'd stay with you and wait for the next train, but you could say I'm working from home this weekend. I gotta get back to Ma."

"She's baking some more?" I say, wearing my most sympathetic face.

"Nah. I told her I'd teach her how to play cards. I figure, if she loses all her money gambling, at least she's not burning the house down, right?"

Too true.

Still, I can't help but wish that when I return home tonight after Shannon's party, someone other than Blue picks me up.

I wind up waiting on the platform for a full hour for the next train, freezing the whole time. Even though it's only October, and even though the day is bright and sunny, it's cold in this tiny tank and gauze top. I should have grabbed a coat at home, and I would have, if I hadn't been in such a hurry to get away from my dad.

But even the cold can't keep me from being excited, and once I'm on the train, I'm even more excited. It helps that the trains are cleaner than they used to be, the bathroom floor not covered with urine that'll stick to my heels when I duck in to take a nervous pee.

It seems to take forever, or no time at all, before I'm pushed out of the train by the tide of passengers behind me, pushed by the tide over the concrete walkway and up the flights of stairs, into the middle of Grand Central Station.

Grand Central Station!

This is *my* town, *my* city, and as I look up at the green ceiling of Grand Central Station, the stars in the zodiac constellations twinkling overhead, for the first time in what seems like forever I feel like I'm *home*.

There's my zodiac: Cancer. And there's Mom's: Capricorn.

Home.

Then some rushing pedestrian in too much of a hurry to get where he's going nearly knocks me off my feet. Back when I still lived here, that would've bothered me. But today it doesn't. People rushing too fast to get where they want to go is just part of New York City. It's part of home.

But much as I'd like to stand here staring at the ceiling all day, much as I'd like to keep getting nearly knocked off my feet just to remind me how happy I am to be here, I have my own places to rush off to, and off I rush.

· · ·

Except, since I didn't even tell Shannon I was coming, I don't need to rush *that* quickly.

So I do something I've been dying to do for months: I *shop*.

Oh, sure, I've been to the Danbury Fair Mall plenty of times since I moved to Hat City, but that's not the same as shopping on Fifth Avenue in Manhattan. It's not the same as trying on five-hundred-dollar pairs of embroidered jeans, only to shrug to the salesgirl afterward, as if to say, *Maybe next week. I think I'm in more of a Jimmy Choo mood today.*

But, as fun as the five-hundred-dollar pairs of jeans are—I mean, you've gotta love all that floral hand-embroidery—I'm not really shopping for myself today. I'm shopping for my best friend, Shannon.

So I go into a florist shop and buy an exotic arrangement, filled with all her favorite colors: pink, purple, yellow, and white; Shannon doesn't really like green, but how can you get a bouquet without any green? There are always going to be some stems, you know? And then I hop into a Japanese chocolate shop. Sure, Shannon's always dieting. Who isn't? But who can resist these chocolates, each miniature one shaped like a different sports car, each one stuffed with fillings like praline, hazelnut, raspberry, and, well, chocolate?

Okay, so maybe it might seem a bit odd, bringing flowers and chocolates to another girl. But you have to remember, this is Shannon we're talking about. Not only is Shannon my best friend, but Shannon also loves pretty and expensive things, plus pretty expensive things. And I was not raised by wolves; I was raised by my mom. And while she may have been killed by J. K. Rowling, before she died, she told me, like, a million times that you never go visiting empty-handed.

And as I shop for nice things for her, each time I pull out my AmEx card, I think of my best friend, Shannon. I daydream the whole while about how wonderful it will be to see her again and I know exactly how the day will go.

When she answers the door and sees me standing there, she'll squeal with delight. She'll jump up and down and clap her hands. I'll tell her to stop acting like a seal, but then I won't be able to help myself. I'll hug her, hard. Then I'll help her get ready for the party, help with the decorations and food, help her pick out what to wear. While we're doing that, she'll notice something different about me. Even though I'll be having a great time with her, being my best friend, she'll see that, under the surface joy, something is troubling me. I am, after all, at least at the moment, a tragic heroine. Shannon will put her arm around my shoulders, she'll lead me to her room, lock the door behind us, put her hands on her hips, and say, *Spill.* And I will. I'll spill. I'll tell her everything. All about how I don't really fit in in Danbury, all about how I like Jack but I'm pretty sure he likes Farrin. But she'll know that's not all, and she'll press me, so I'll tell her all about my dad being FDA, Sex Pervert Extraordinaire. Then she'll do The Perfect Shannon Thing: She'll give me a strong hug, and while she's doing that, she'll solve all my problems. She'll tell me exactly the right thing to do to solve and resolve the situation with my dad. She'll make me feel better, about everything. She'll help me to stop being Hamlet.

Then she'll help me plot how to get Todd back.

That's exactly the way it will be.

Except it isn't like that at all.

How come nothing is ever the way I expect it to be?

Oh, it starts out well enough, with Shannon's mother answering the door, answering the door to her Park Avenue duplex apartment in New York City. Park Avenue duplex apartment in New York City! Sorry, but now that I live in Danbury, I love saying things like that.

Shannon's mother is like an older, surgeried version of Shannon, her dyed blond hair in a thick ponytail tied off with a Hermès scarf—Hermès might have refused to stay open late for Oprah, but no store ever closes its doors to Stella Steel—her hangerlike body encircled in one of those wrap dresses that have blinding patterns on them and a sash at the side. On her feet? If those aren't the Famous Shoes from the very first episode of *Sex and the City*, the electric purple Jimmy Choo sandals with the Swarovski crystal thong, I'll eat my AmEx Gold Card. So, okay, with all the different colors and patterns on her, she looks like a goose. But, hey, at least she's an *expensive* goose.

"Mrs. Steel!" I shout, throwing my arms around her. "You're so . . . *skinny*!" I mean, she is skinny, she's always been skinny, but now she's skinni*er*. She's scary skinny now, and I can feel the fragile bag of bones her body is made up of as I hug her. But still, as I hug her I compliment her again on her skinniness, knowing this is the one thing I can say that'll make her happiest. Sure, it's like hugging a wire monkey, but in this moment she's the closest thing to a mother I've got.

"Shannon never said you were, er, *coming*," Mrs. Steel says, peeling me off her. Okay, so maybe she really is like a wire monkey and not at all like any kind of mother I'd want to have.

My own mother would never make one of her daughter's friends feel even the slightest bit unwelcome. My own mother would never wear such a horrid combination of clashing clothes. And if my own mother ever did dye her hair, it would *not* come out *yellow*.

"I'm sorry," I apologize stiffly. "Perhaps I should have called first?"

Mrs. Steel's expression softens as she says, "Oh, no, of course not, dear. Why would a friend ever need to call first?" But when she says this last, a strange thing happens: She looks as though she feels sorry for me.

Why should Mrs. Steel feel sorry for me? I mean, outside of all of the obvious reasons.

"May I come in, then?" I say, reverting to the not-raised-by-wolves manners my mother instilled in me.

I see the struggle in Mrs. Steel's eyes. Is she actually considering turning me away?

"Of course, dear," she says, stepping back to finally let me enter, as though I'm that count in that Bram Stoker book when, let me tell you, she's the one who looks like Dracula right now. "If that's what you want," she says.

Well, of course it's what I *want*. Why else would I have taken two cabs and one train, waiting forever for good transportation? Why else would I have shown up on her doorstep with candy and chocolates if I did *not* want to be let in?

I step in, onto the high-polish tiled floor in the foyer, the huge black-and-white tiles swirling like a gigantic chessboard all around me. I grew up on that floor. Well, practically. With Mom and Dad both being writers, and with writers needing a certain amount of quiet in order to, well, *write*, during our really young days Shannon and I spent much more time playing at the Steel home than at my place. This is the floor where I first skated in stocking feet. This is the floor where I first realized that Hot Wheels could be as much fun as dolls, thanks to Shannon's two-years-older brother, Shane. This is the floor where I first realized I was never going to look like Polly Pocket.

And I am standing on that giant chessboard of a floor, about to start up the iron circular staircase, hand poised over the post, when I hear Shannon laugh, loud; when I see Shannon, in stocking feet, skid to a stop on the slippery natural wood boards at the top of the staircase, in the hallway of the floor just above. I know that floor is slippery because it always is, the whole damn apartment is—Shannon and I having stocking-skated it often enough.

Omigod, it's Shannon! It's *Shannon*! And with her natural blond hair swinging behind her like a hair commercial, her eyes sparkling like the sky outside, she looks better than I even remembered. She definitely looks happier than I remembered. And skinnier too, her body covered in what can only be described as a black catsuit. Not scary skinny like her mom, but like she could be if she's not careful, like maybe she's about to have too much of a good thing. Still . . .

"Shannon!" I scream up to her.

And that's when she stops laughing.

I hear a guy's voice from the upper floor, yelling something like "I got you now!" but I don't pay it any heed, my mind probably figuring it must be Shane. I don't pay it any heed because I'm so puzzled, watching the expressions change so quickly on Shannon's face, changing so fast that I don't even have time to name them all.

Then the guy who matches the voice skids into view, catching Shannon by the waist from behind. And as he buries his face in her neck, all I can see is the blond top of his head. But that's all I need to see. I know that blond head.

"Todd?" Even though I know who it is, I say it just like that anyway, like it's a question.

At the same time I say "Todd?" Shannon says "Ren?" and Todd says "Ren?"

I instantly feel bitter. Even though I've started liking Jack, started liking him very much, I am still bitter.

I block Shannon out of the picture, focus my attention down to a narrow dime on Todd.

When you think about it, anything that's wrong in the world can be laid at the feet of someone named Todd.

"Wow," I say, "you broke it off with Sheila already?"

Todd looks shocked. "Sheila?" He looks from me to Shannon, puzzled. He shakes his head. "I was never with Sheila."

And in that instant, for the first time, I see everything clearly. Shannon never meant to invite me to her party tonight. She invited me only after I told her about Kiki's invitation, when she was sure I wouldn't, couldn't come.

I drop the flowers and chocolates at the foot of the stairs in the chessboard foyer and run for the door.

Before, earlier today, I fleed—flew?—to get here, and now I'm doing the exact opposite. I cannot get away fast enough.

Shannon catches up with me halfway down the block, where I'm standing on the sidewalk, hand raised, trying to hail a cab as the tears run down my face. Even though it's chilly out, I register that Shannon is still in her stocking feet.

"You weren't supposed to find out like this!" she cries, grabbing my arm.

"Maybe I was never supposed to find out," I say, trying to shrug her off.

But her grip is strong. "No." She shakes her head, as though trying to convince herself as much as me. "I would have told you . . . eventually . . . when the time was right."

"When would the time be right, Shannon, huh? When would the time be right for you to tell me you started going out with the guy you knew I still liked?"

"Look," she says, "he probably never would have stopped going out with you if you'd been willing to do what he wanted."

"Oh," I say, "and you *are* willing to do it? Is that supposed to make everything all right somehow?"

She doesn't say anything to that.

"You told me that you were going out with Rick and that Todd was going out with Sheila now," I say, "but it was you with Todd all along, wasn't it? You just said all that other stuff to create some kind of diversion, figuring I'd never find out."

She doesn't say anything to that, either, and right then a cab pulls up beside me, cabdrivers everywhere being the patron saints of lost girls from Connecticut, and I'm in.

But there is no comfort in cabs today. There is no comfort in anything. There is no comfort in the people rushing rushing rushing outside the window, there is no comfort in the zodiac signs twinkling on the green ceiling over Grand Central Station, there is no comfort in the clean Metro-North train speeding me backward, no comfort anywhere as I race to reverse the process begun earlier in the day.

There is, I finally think during the train ride back, one glimmer of hope. If I can just race fast enough, I should get back to Danbury's train station in time to catch a cab to Kiki's party. If I'm lucky, there'll be a chance for me to see my real friends tonight.

If they'll still have me.

George unlocks the backseat passenger door from inside but doesn't get out to hold the door for me. Unlike Mohammed, who has manners enough to work for the queen of England, and unlike Blue, who is suddenly practicing for a job as a professional chauffeur, George drives a cab strictly to get out of the house for a few hours at a time. He always says he loves his wife tremendously, but enough is enough.

"She's the best woman the good Lord ever made," he always says, his goatee keeping some kind of weird rhythm in time with his pronounced lisp, "and Lord knows she can cook to beat the devil"—whatever that means—"but if I want to watch a TV show, she's got to watch it with me, even if it's something she hates. If I *do* try to take up a hobby, like golf, and then I actually try to *play* golf, she's got to learn too. If I didn't have my time in the cab here, I'd get *no* rest."

"Where's Blue?" I ask, climbing in. It not being a weekday before six, the time George does work, and it being a weekend, when Blue always works, it's a genuine puzzle.

"Aw," he says, "her and her ma got so caught up playing cards today, they decided to take off for that Atlantic City. So she asked me to cover for her."

Well, that explains that at least.

"Plus," George goes on, "if I stayed home, Martha was going to make me clean out the kitchen cabinets with her, and I don't *do* Lysol."

There was that, too.

"Yeah," I say, trying to sympathize, "Lysol can be a real . . . *bitch*." But my voice catches on that last word—"bitch"—because all I can do when I say it is think of Shannon, my former best friend.

George's warm brown eyes study me in the rearview mirror, and I hope that in the dark he can't see the tears forming in my eyes. "Yeah"—he says the word slowly—"Lysol always has that effect on me too. Every time I even say the word, it just makes me want to cry."

And at that, even though I try to stop it, a sob escapes.

"Okay," George says, his voice smooth and soothing like chocolate now, even in spite of the lisp, "I know this can't all be about Lysol. Even I don't get that upset about Lysol. Tell your uncle George what's going on."

At the sweet idea of him being my uncle George, another sob escapes, because someone feeling as sorry for you as you do for yourself always makes you feel sappier. But then, in the same instant, the thought of him as my uncle George just seems funny, and the sob sort of turns into a laugh, the half sob/half laugh coming out as a squeak.

"Okay, now I really know it's not all about Lysol. I never make that sound about Lysol. In fact, the only time I make that sound is when Martha tells me it's time to clean out the garage. Or the attic. Or my sock drawer. Or—"

And now I can't help it. I'm laughing full-out.

"That's good," George soothes, pulling up in front of Kiki's house in Ridgefield. "That's good. So we've established it's definitely not about the damn Lysol."

I'm laughing so hard now that it's turning into tears again, not least because I've never heard George, who always talks respectfully about "the good Lord," swear before.

"Well," George finally concludes, this time getting out of his seat to open my door for me, which just goes to show how kind he's trying to be, "if it's not the Lysol, it's got to be one of two things: It's either a problem with love or a problem with money."

I hand George a wad of cash, throwing in more than my usual extra, for the distance driven and the compassion shown.

George looks from the wad in his hand to the house in front of us.

Kiki's house is a mansion with a stone gate, a long slate walkway to the front door, and a big solid oak door that looks like it was stolen from a castle. The house itself sprawls out in all directions, the color a burnt orangey-yellowy brown, burnt sienna I think it's called, something very Italian looking, like maybe Leonardo da Vinci knocked this off between painting chapel ceilings and creating the code. All the windows of the house are lit up with individual candles, like the people who live there are expecting the whole world to come tonight.

Then George looks back from the house to the wad in his hand.

"Okay." He smiles, the moonlight glinting off a gold dogtooth I never even noticed before. "One thing we know for sure: The problem sure isn't with money."

•   •   •

A servant wearing an actual maid's uniform answers the door.

A gorgeous woman whose caramel-colored sweater dress matches the color of her skin comes into view behind the maid. I suddenly have a vision of what Kiki will look like twenty-five years from now: Kiki will be stunning.

"Omigod," I shriek, shrinking back involuntarily. "I thought you were dead!"

The woman in question is, of course, Lili Rodriguez, Kiki's mother and soap opera star. The only problem is, her character is dead. Well, she's supposedly dead, unless her character is about to come out of Nikos's deep-freeze room as one of the *un*dead. Or maybe the writers will just make it all a bad dream. My mom said they did that once on a nighttime soap she used to watch as a kid—made a whole season turn out to be a bad dream so they could bring a character back from the dead—and that was the last time she watched a soap. On the other hand, my mom also said they did that at the end of a whole comedy series she used to watch, and she just loved it. So there you have it, folks: Sometimes it's good to use the it-was-all-a-bad-dream device, sometimes it's bad. Take your pick.

All I know is, right now I'm feeling really bad. I'm feeling bad because, possibly as an overflow from the weird and awful day I'm having, I just said something inexcusably rude to Kiki's mother. I accused her of being dead!

"Omigod," I say again. "I'm so sorry, I'm so so sorry. I didn't mean to say that. It just . . . slipped out."

"It's okay." She laughs, and her smile is so wide, I know she means it. "Do you have any idea how often I get that? Honestly, I've been dead on that show so many times and come back again, even *I* don't know which one I am anymore!"

I laugh along with her, glad the awkward moment I created has passed, and we enjoy a shared-chuckle moment.

Of course, all good things, like chuckle moments, must come to an end, and this one does when Lili Rodriquez says, a slight frown furrowing her pretty brow, "By the way, who are you?"

"Yes." I laugh nervously, back to being my awkward self. "That would help, wouldn't it?" How lame can I get? "I'm Ren D'Arc?" I ask/answer. "In Kiki's class at Waylord?"

"Oh, right," she says after a moment, the light dawning. "I read all of both your parents' books."

That's always nice to hear.

"I was sorry to hear about your mom."

That, too.

She shakes her head in sympathy. "That J. K. Rowling, huh?"

Yup. That makes two of us.

"So, Kiki is expecting you?" It's not a bad question about someone expecting you, not like Mrs. Steel's was. In fact, there's something open and inviting about it, but still . . .

And we're back to that square one, where things are never so good.

"Well, yes, she was," I say. "I mean, she invited me, and I said I could and would, but then I didn't think I could, so I said I couldn't and wouldn't, but then something else happened, and now, well"—helpless shrug at the occasional idiocy that is me—"I'm here."

"All *righty*, then," Lili Rodriguez says, eyeing me with the kind of back-stepping look usually reserved for the kookies that aren't all safely locked in the kookie jar. Then she does a face-scrunching smile/grimace at me. "Maybe I should just get Kiki. They're down in the basement." She reaches for a knob on a door that is across from the entryway. As soon as she opens it, a blast of loud music hits me in the face. Dido? Sheryl Crow? Macy Gray? I can never keep any of them straight. I just know the names.

I move to follow her.

"Oh, no, no," she says, that smile still desperately

bright. "You can wait in the living room over there." She gives a nod with her chin. "I'll just go tell Kiki you're here."

So this is the house that *All My Days of Restless Passion* built, I'm thinking as I look around the living room where Lili has indicated I should wait. The high heels of my shoes sink into the deep-pile, cream-colored carpet, and there are a whole bunch of conversational arrangements of chairs and couches, all plush in deep browns and reds. On the walls are pieces of art that look like they were painted by someone important. Jutting out from the middle of a fieldstone fireplace that takes up almost an entire wall is a mantelpiece, on which all of Lili's awards rest. There are three *Soap Opera Digest* awards and four Emmys. I pick up one of the latter and heft it over my head in a victory gesture. "Take *that*, Susan Lucci," I say, pretending I'm accepting my own award before switching into Leo DiCaprio mode. "I'm queen of the soaps!"

"Put the Emmy down and no one gets hurt," I hear T'Keyah's familiar, rich voice say behind me.

I put the Emmy down. Believe me, you would have put it down too.

Still, when I turn, I expect to see a laugh in T'Keyah's eyes, but there's none there. She looks great in a black halter top and jeans. And beside her Kiki looks like they must have gone shopping together, wearing a white halter top with the same jeans. Only, of course, they're not the exact same pair of jeans, since they're on her.

"You both look fantastic!" I say, meaning it.

"What. Are. You. Doing. Here." That's T'Keyah, enunciating.

Well, that was warm.

"Yeah," says Kiki, "we thought you had some fire-hot plans in the city. You know, the Big City?"

It's funny how sometimes you can hear it when someone is talking in capital letters, isn't it?

I shrug. I'm pretty sure that, if I could only see myself right now, I'd look just like Max the dog in *How the Grinch Stole Christmas*.

"I decided to come here instead?" I wince.

"I'm not buying it," T'Keyah says.

"Me either," says Kiki. "I think something went wrong. I think the reason you're here is because something went drastically wrong at That Other Party."

And then there are times when you can hear someone talking in capital letters and it's just not funny at all.

Like right then. Which is exactly when I burst into tears. And not just delicate tears, like when Shannon caught me up on the sidewalk, and not a sob that turns into a squeal, like what happened with George. No, these are big honking sobs. These are the honkingest sobs I've let out since my mother died.

"Oh, shit," Kiki says. Through my blurry tears, I see her grab something glittery off the mantel, then she thrusts one of her mother's Emmys at me. "Here. Take it, take it."

"You can't just give Crazypants one of your mother's Emmys!" T'Keyah cries.

"She's not wearing pants." Kiki eyes my skort. "Is that what you people wear to New York parties?" she snidely asks me before turning back to T'Keyah. "And of course I'm not giving her one of Mama's Emmys. But look at Crazyskort: She's *crying*. I can't just let her keep on *crying* like that."

Crazypants; Crazyskort. Gee, they were making me feel better by the minute.

"Besides," Kiki goes on, still talking to T'Keyah as if I'm not even there, "you know what always happens to me when other people cry."

"You cry too," T'Keyah says. And suddenly, I see there's a tear in T'Keyah's eye too.

"*Yes!*" Kiki bawls, putting her arms around T'Keyah.

"Which is why you can never watch your mother on TV," T'Keyah says, blubbering herself now. "Every time she cries, you cry!"

"Especially when she dies!" Kiki adds.

"Um, guys?" I say. "I mean, girls? Remember me?"

"That's right," T'Keyah says, "you started this."

At first I think she's accusing me, but just like earlier, when I was wrong in thinking that she was just joking about putting down the Emmy, I'm wrong about this as well. I see T'Keyah and Kiki open up their embrace just enough to allow me in.

We are now a circle of three.

"So, what was it?" T'Keyah says, the first of our triangular circle to gain control of herself. "What was it that set you off crying? Surely, it can't be me. I mean, I'm not *that* scary."

I almost tell her, *Yes, sometimes you are.* But this is such a female bonding moment, I don't want to spoil it. And, anyway, there are more important things going on.

So I start to open my mouth to tell them about Todd, about Shannon, but I suddenly realize that's not the most important thing going on in my life right now. That's over. I may still be feeling stuff about it, but it's over. This thing with my dad, on the other hand, is still going on. In many ways, it's just starting.

So then I open my mouth to tell them about my dad, but then I shut it again real quick. As good as I feel in this moment with them, after just getting burned bad by Shannon, I just can't trust my new friends with something this huge. Not yet.

"Um, uh, um, uh." T'Keyah mimics me. "Are you trying to catch flies, Ren?" she says. At least she's back to calling me Ren. I hated it when she and Kiki sounded like Farrin. "Are you some kind of frog?"

See what I mean about her being kind of scary?

"Spit it *out*," T'Keyah commands.

And I do, spilling everything about Todd and Shannon.

"I knew it would have something to do with someone named Todd," T'Keyah says.

"That Shannon doesn't deserve you," Kiki says.

They are really so good, so *solid*, that I think maybe—

"Kiki?" Lili Rodriguez yells. "Don't you think you should spend some time with your other guests? You do have a basement full of people you invited downstairs. I was just down there, and Michael Houseman was asking for you."

"Michael Houseman?" I say. "Isn't that Mouse? But he's such a stoner. What's he doing down in your basement? And why would your mother be telling you he's asking for you?" A thought occurs to me. Well, I did tell you I was intuitive, right? "You're not going out with him, are you?" If I weren't so busy talking, I'd be speechless.

"Oh," Kiki pooh-poohs me, thankfully not taking offense, "he's not stoned *all* the time."

"See what I'm talking about?" T'Keyah leans in toward me as we trail Kiki down the basement stairs. "Any old time there's trouble or girls crying, there's always a guy involved."

True, I think. Well, except for when people are lesbians.

No sooner do we get down the stairs to Kiki's basement—a totally cool room with rainbow-colored ceiling and floor, giant throw pillows to sit on all over the place, and a sound system that would make the whole neighborhood deaf if not for the wraparound white leather soundproofing, meaning it's only making everyone in the basement deaf—than Kiki sidles over to Mouse, whose longish blond hair looks cleaner than usual and whose green eyes look less red-rimmed than usual, making for a less startling Christmas motif than usual. For as long as I've known him, which I'll admit has not been for very long, whenever I look at Mouse, I mostly think that if they could just plug him into a socket at Wal-Mart, they could sell thousands of him as a holiday decoration. But tonight he doesn't look too bad. He doesn't necessarily look good, but he really doesn't look too bad. Maybe, I think, Kiki is right, and maybe Mouse is less stoned than usual.

And then, of course, the burning question still remains. . . .

"He's really not that bad!" T'Keyah shouts into my ear, her response to my previous question of "What the hell does Kiki see in Mouse?"

"When you get to know him, he's kind of nice!" T'Keyah yells some more.

One thing I look forward to about getting older is listening to music at volumes loud enough to enjoy it but without going deaf or having to shout. Just don't tell anyone I said that, okay?

"In fact," T'Keyah shouts, "if you want to do even more to get on Kiki's good side, you might consider calling him Michael! Kiki's got her own little campaign going to get everyone to stop calling him Mouse!"

Kiki was organizing an entire campaign? How come I never know these things?

"Because you're always too obsessed with your own shit!" T'Keyah answers when I say as much to her. "It's not always about you you you—you know?"

Huh. Maybe she had something there.

Suddenly, I'm worried about Kiki. "Does she get stoned with Mouse a lot?" I shout. "I mean, Michael?"

"Nah. She tried it a few times, but it just makes her sick, plus she says it makes her feel stupid, even before she gets sick. As a matter of fact, that's the main reason Michael's cutting back. He's doing it for Kiki!"

How romantic.

"Are you going to be okay by yourself?" T'Keyah shouts. "There's someone I need to go talk to!"

"Who?"

"Him!" She nods with her chin. And I see a gorgeous black guy, talking to some other guys I know are on the basketball team. He's taller than the others, and they're all hanging on his words like he's a god or something.

"Who is he?"

"Marcus Dawson! You know? *The captain of the team?*"

Why didn't I know that?

"Marcus Dawson! You know? *My boyfriend?*"

How did I not know that Kiki was hooking up with Michael Mouse and that T'Keyah has a boyfriend?

Maybe T'Keyah's right. Maybe I am too self-involved.

Does everyone except me have a boyfriend?

While I'm ruminating on all of that, T'Keyah takes the opportunity to slink away, sidling up to Marcus. It seems like everyone in the room is slinking and sidling except for me. I want to slink! I want to sidle!

And even though the basement is large, it's packed full of kids from Waylord. Now that the protective cover of T'Keyah is gone, I see, in addition to most of the basketball players from both the boys' and girls' teams, most of the cheerleading squad and most everyone from my homeroom. Even Dylan Zimmerman is there.

Who can I slink and sidle up to?

Certainly not Dylan Zimmerman.

I start cautiously moving around the room. If you were watching me from the outside, it might look like I'm checking everyone out, as if the decision of whom to talk to is all mine. But in reality, we all know—okay, maybe everyone in that room doesn't know yet, because maybe most if not all of them are just as self-involved as I am, but you and I know—I'm looking for one person. I'm looking for Jack.

"Lose something, twerp?" I hear the dulcet tones of Farrin Farraway's voice shout in my ear. "Or are you looking for something?"

I don't even turn to look at her, because there in the corner is Jack.

At the same time he sees me.

"Hey, Ren!" he shouts. He's even smiling. "I didn't know you were coming tonight!"

Farrin sidles right on past me, puts her hand in the

crook of Jack's arm. "C'mon," she says to him, and in the semidark room I can see she's all gold and white: strapless blinding-white dress, snug enough to read the lettering on a dime if she had a dime under her dress, gold jewelry, gold high-heeled sandals that make my own look like flats, gold hair tied back in a big white ribbon, and skin dyed too gold from too much time in the tanning bed.

Okay, so I'm catty.

Jack is still looking at me when Farrin repeats, "C'mon, Jack. Come keep me company while I warm up the car."

Gross!

He shrugs at me as if to say, *What can I do?* Then he lets her lead him away. But as she brushes by me just close enough so I can hear her, she talks into my ear: "Just don't screw up the pyramid on Tuesday, D'Arc, or it'll be the last game you'll ever cheer at."

How could I have forgotten the first basketball game of the year on Tuesday? The one where I'm supposed to make my debut as the pinnacle of the pyramid?

I'm screwed.

More important than that, Jack's gone.

"You really like him, don't you?" T'Keyah shouts, startling me out of my Jack reverie.

In fact, I'm so startled, I don't have time to erect the

usual block I put up between my head/heart and my mouth, and so I simply blurt out, "Yes!"

"Well, don't sweat it. Ever since Farrin got that Mini Cooper of hers, she always drives Jack places. It doesn't mean anything."

Maybe not to her, but to me it's just the last in a line of awful things in a day that, despite its few high points, has been mostly awful. First, I catch Shannon with Todd. Now Jack, for whatever reason, has gone off with Farrin. It has, finally, been too much of a day.

"I gotta go," I say to T'Keyah. I look over to where Kiki is panning for gold with her tongue in Mouse/Michael's mouth. "Tell Kiki good-bye and thanks for me, okay?"

"Sure!" she says. "But why not stay for a bit? Meet some new people? Or get to know the people you've already met better?"

"Not tonight!" I yell. "Another time!"

It's weird to be shouting so loud when I'm feeling so depressed. Usually, I try to reserve shouting for joy or anger, but the music compels me to scream like a psychotic.

"But how will you get home?" T'Keyah asks.

"Cab!" I say, suddenly feeling the full loneliness of my life. "I'll cab it!"

. . .

Miracle of miracles and God be praised, even though I'm twenty minutes from Danbury, even though Helena answered when I called Wheels Instead of Heels, it takes only twenty minutes for the cab to get to me. In the meantime, I've thanked Lili Rodriguez for the hospitality of her home, hefted one of her Emmys one last time, finally peed, and spent the remainder of the time in front of the house, gazing up at the night sky, wishing my mom had been right when I was young: that if I just wished upon the brightest star, my wish might come true.

Not only miracle of miracles, but surprise, surprise and praise Allah, too: It being a weekend, Blue should be driving the cab, but since George replaced her earlier, I thought he'd be the one to come get me. Yet it's Mohammed who pulls up, my favorite in the bunch.

"Miss Ren," he says, "you do not have a hat."

I pat myself on the head, confirming the absence of any hat. "You guessed right on the first try," I say, climbing into the back. "I just want to go home."

He lifts up his skullcap, offering it to me as he's done in the past. "Is this where I am supposed to say, 'Here is your hat? What is your hurry?'"

I'm barely able to muster a smile in return.

"You really should have worn a hat tonight, Miss Ren. It is cold out, getting colder."

"Tomorrow I'll wear a hat, Mohammed." I sigh.

"What is wrong, Miss Ren?"

"Life, Mohammed, life."

"Ah. I know that song and dance. I have been there and I have done that and I even have the T-shirt to prove it."

When I walk in the door, the downstairs lights are still on. My dad is still up, an eventuality I have not anticipated.

I take off my shoes, tiptoe to the kitchen. I grab a can of Diet Pepsi Vanilla from the refrigerator, then reach for a packet of Frosted Chocolate Fudge Pop-Tarts in the cabinet, my stomach rumbling to tell me I haven't eaten in hours. When did I eat today? Have I had anything since breakfast? No wonder I feel so grumpy. *Must be low blood sugar,* I decide, so I grab the whole box instead. Sure, there's a thousand calories right there, maybe twelve hundred, but who's counting? Given what I've eaten today, or lack thereof, this practically qualifies as being on a diet. In my zeal to get to my Pop-Tarts as quickly as possible, I close the cabinet too abruptly, making a banging sound, and my dad calls out, "Ren?"

Okay, he knows I'm in the house. He knows I'm in the kitchen. So I can't very well just go right up to my room without saying anything. It's awful to feel this dread. I never felt this way about my dad before, and now it's practically all I feel.

I slunk over to his office, "slunk" being the depressed and slumping form of "slink."

"Yeah," I say, trying to muster the warmth I used to feel whenever he'd let me interrupt his work; the times, as a child, when he'd let me climb into his lap, even though he was working on some kind of big important novel, and he'd let me go to places on his computer like www.StrawberryShortcake.com, letting me read about the characters or play games like the butterfly-catching game or even flip through the shop for all the things I wished I could have.

And in that moment, leaning against the open door to his office, thinking about the past, I *do* feel warm toward my dad. But then I see where he is sitting—right in front of the computer screen, the dreaded computer screen—and all the bad feelings come back.

What is he doing on the computer? Is he talking to someone online? And if he is, whom is he talking to? Is he FDA'ing some poor innocent girl?

"Um, what are you doing?" I say.

"Just working on a chapter for my book," he says, taking off his reading glasses. His eyes look tired. "I couldn't sleep until you got home, so I figured I might as well make myself useful, get some work done."

I'm tempted to walk behind his black leather chair, look at the screen myself to see exactly what he's up to. But it's hard to make my feet move in that direction. And when I'm finally able to, no sooner do I take that first step than he switches the computer off. In a way, it's a relief.

"Bedtime for both of us?" he says.

"I guess."

He crosses the room, studying my face closer than he has in a long time.

"Is something wrong, Ren? You don't seem yourself."

Of course I'm not myself! my brain shouts. *How can I be myself anymore with everything else that's going on?* But hard on the heels of that thought comes another: *If I'm no longer myself, the person I used to know, who am I?*

"I'm fine," I say. I won't—*can't*—explain it to him. "It's just been a really long day."

In my room, the door safely closed, I look out the curtains at the moon. I go to open the box of Pop-Tarts only to find I'm no longer hungry. If there's an upside to my life falling completely apart, perhaps it'll be that for the first time in my life I'll finally be perfectly thin.

I crack open my Diet Pepsi, because even if hunger is no longer an issue, thirst certainly is, and I turn on my computer. When it boots up, I see five e-mails from

Shannon, a bunch of spam, and an e-mail from Sex World informing me I have a private message. Do I want to receive it? No, I do not. But I click on the link anyway, and there he is:

From: FDA
To: SexGurl1

I don't know about you, honey, but I can't stop counting the hours between now and Friday night. Hell, I'm starting to count the minutes. Even the seconds! By my calculations, there are approximately five hundred and eighteen thousand, four hundred minutes until we meet. Maybe more. Maybe less. Mathematics was never my strong suit. Words, as you may have guessed, are more my thing. Can you feel it? Can you feel the excitement? Are you counting the days, hours, minutes, seconds until we meet? I can't wait to meet you, to finally see you and hold you in my arms.

Your Guy,
FDA

My skin begins to crawl, but I force myself to write back:

From: SexGurl1
To: FDA

Sure. I can't wait.

And although I can bring myself to do that, I can't bring myself to sign it "Your Girl" before punching send, even though I know that's a touch he would like. I just can't.

When I'm done, I turn the computer off. It's a gentle enough gesture when what I really want to do is rip out the wires and throw the computer out the window, rip out the wires of all computers in the world and throw them all in the trash.

But, of course, I can't do that. I can't get rid of mine because I need to see how this all turns out. I can't get rid of all the rest of the computers in the world because I simply don't have that much power.

So I do the only thing I can do. I kick off my shoes, flop down on the bed, crawl under the covers still fully clothed, and try my damnedest to go to sleep.

And so ends the longest day—and night!—ever.

From: Shannongirl@yaahoo.com
To: RenD@aaol.com

R,

No, that's too casual for us now. Let me start again.

Ren,

I am so sorry you caught me with Todd on Saturday. I wish you hadn't. I am so, so sorry. Please let me make it up to you?

Luv
S
I mean: Love, Shannon

Let her make it up to me? Yeah, right. In a pig's ear, which is exactly what I'd say if I were given to using trite old sayings. So instead, I'll just say: No way, bitch.

Except I'm too shy to write it.

Too shy? No, that's not the right word. In Jo-Jo's class he talks sometimes about the Sherlock Holmes character in Arthur Conan Doyle's mysteries as being jaded. Yeah, that's me now: jaded. Except I'm not like, you know, an opium addict.

I mean, look at what Shannon writes. She doesn't say she's sorry she got involved with Todd in the first place. Oh, no. She says she's sorry I *caught* her with him. Big difference there: not "sorry I did it," just "sorry I got caught." That's like Bonnie and Clyde or something: *We'd keep robbing banks forever if the law-man didn't done come and kill us.* Don't look that up in the history books. I made that up. I don't know what they talked like, but I'm pretty sure they didn't done talk with that "didn't done" crap I put in their mouths. But I'm also pretty sure that if they'd never been caught and killed, they would have happily kept on keeping on, robbing more banks, killing a person here and there along the way.

Which is exactly why I'm not going to answer this dumb e-mail Shannon has tainted my inbox with. Because I'm hurt. Because I'm jaded. Because I'm angry as all get-out.

But that idea of people going on doing bad things until they get caught has got me thinking. Now that

I've got Farrin out of my dad's clutches, even though I'm temporarily in them as Fake Farrin, that can't go on forever. I have to keep reminding myself: If I don't find a way to take my own dad out of commission—and, no, I'm not talking about killing him here—he'll just eventually move on to someone else. If Farrin doesn't get hurt, someone else eventually will. There's a horrible thought: *Someone else will eventually get hurt . . . if they haven't already.*

Omigod, that's not just a horrible thought. It's a *chilling* thought. But how can I stop more bad things from happening? And who can help me figure out exactly what to do?

There is only one person left whom I trust 100 percent.

Dear Mom,

Everything is just so awful since you've been gone, and it just gets worse all the time.

Remember when I was little? Remember when I was five or six and I used to worry about you dying? You'd tuck me in at night and say the magic words; you'd say, "Everyone in this house loves you." (Even though it wasn't really a house; it was a duplex.) You'd say, "Your father and I love you more than anything in the whole wide world." (which was a nice touch.) And then together we'd say, "Direct my steps for good in this world, all the days of my life." (Because you and Dad were never much on organized religion.) Well, that was all fine until I turned five or six. Then I started being aware of people dying. I'd see it on TV. It'd happen in kids' families at school, a grandparent here, an aunt or uncle there. And then Grandma died, and sad as I was to lose her, I suddenly realized: She was <u>your</u> <u>mother</u>! And if your mother could die, then, someday, my mother could die.

It was just awful. I was more scared of that happening than I'd ever been of anything in my life before. More scared than of spiders. Way more scared than of snakes. Even more scared than I was of that crazy lady next door who used to yell at me for just being a loudly happy kid.

And what was I so scared of? All kinds of little-kid things. I was scared of no one being around to cut the crust off my bread just right. I was scared of no one being around who'd tie my shoelaces for me when I was too tired to tie them straight. Mostly, I was scared of being left alone in this world without one half of the two people

in the house who loved me, scared of being left
alone in this world without one half of the two
people who loved me more than anything in the
whole wide world, scared of being left alone in
this world without one half of the two people
who were supposed to help me learn how to direct
my steps for good in this world, all the days of
my life.

Well—I snort here—as it turns out, Dad's
not going to be much help with <u>that</u> last item.

Do you remember now what you used to
say to me when I'd get so scared?

Even if you don't, I remember exactly what
you'd say. You'd say, "Close your eyes. Now
picture my face. Can you see me? Now I'm
going to be quiet for a minute and you see if,
with your eyes closed, you can hear the sound
of my voice." Then you'd be quiet for a minute,
and when you started talking again, you'd say,
"Did you hear me in your head? I'll bet if I
weren't in the same room as you, you could
even remember what I smell like. I'll bet if I
weren't here, you'd still remember what that
raw brownie batter we ate too much of, and got
sick together because of, tasted like. I'll bet if
I weren't with you, if you just closed your

eyes for a minute, you could remember exactly what it feels like to have my arms around you. That's the secret of loving people, Ren. When they're not with you in body, you can sense them totally, even if not being with you in body means they're dead. I can't promise you I won't die before you're ready for me to die. No one, not even a parent, can make that promise. But I can promise you that as long as you can see and hear and feel me, in your head and in your heart, I'll always live on for you."

And then you'd go on to say, "And when you know another person, if you really know them like we know each other, you can always imagine what they'd say in any given situation. Like when you say to me, 'I don't want to eat my peas,' and I say back—"

And here I'd jump in, "'There are kids starving in India.'"

"Or if you say, 'Can I have that Polly Pocket pool set?' on a Thursday, and I say back—"

"'Tomorrow's Friday. When you get your allowance tomorrow, you can afford it yourself.'"

"Or if you say, 'Please don't ever die, Mom,' and I say—"

"'It's okay, because even when I die, somehow, I'll always be with you.'"

I heard you then, mom. I just forgot for a while. I hear you now. You're saying I need to somehow find a way to do the right thing, somehow find a way to do good in this world while at the same time taking care of Dad.

I'll do it, mom. I don't know how yet, but, somehow, I'll do it.

And I also hear you telling me that with Dad in trouble and with you not physically here anymore, even though I can always hear you in my head and heart, I need to find someone else <u>in this world</u>, maybe even more than one person, I can trust.

You're right, mom. It's too much now. It's too hard trying to do everything by myself. It's time to let other people in, really in.

I'm sorry you're dead, mom. I'm sorry you're not here. And I'm <u>really</u> sorry J. K. Rowling killed you. But I do want you to know something, mom: I'm going to be okay. Don't ever worry about me, wherever you are, because I love you and I'm going to be okay.

Love,
Ren

Sunday, I spend all day in the house, missing my mom and trying to avoid my dad.

And now it's Monday—Monday!—and I'm excited because I can't wait to go to school.

I also can't believe I just said that—"I can't wait to go to school"—because, I mean, what kind of a teenager am I? But it's just so good to get out of that house, which feels like a tomb to me now.

Sometimes I feel like I'm two people at once. On the one hand, I'm this sad girl, missing her mom and dealing with all this serious stuff. On the other hand, I'm just like everyone else at school, talking all excited like I've eaten too many Frosted Chocolate Fudge Pop-Tarts and worrying about silly stuff, like what everyone thinks of me. I think in two different voices; I even talk in two different voices. But then, I think, isn't everyone really like this? Isn't everyone more complex than just being one kind of person, in just one kind of situation? After all, life is never wholly one thing or another. Life is a constant combination of happy and sad, silly and serious.

Anyway, it's Monday—Monday!—and I'm so excited to be going back to school, to get out of the house, until I go to first-period algebra class and Mrs. Fuchs gives us a pop quiz, pop quizzes being definitely *not* as good as Frosted Chocolate Fudge Pop-Tarts.

Yes, the algebra teacher's name really is Mrs. Fuchs, and she really does make us call her "Mrs." instead of "Ms." Jo-Jo told me, one day when we were talking, that her husband's last name means something innocent like "seal," as in the animal, in the country where they come from. I think they come from Flemland, maybe? But even Jo-Jo agrees, it's downright ridiculous for a teacher of high school students to come to class with a name like Fuchs. I mean, there's so much we can do with that name, it's almost too easy, so mostly we just let it go.

But I can't let the pop quiz go, even though I wish I could. It's just so *hard.* And all the while I'm trying to fill in the answers, trying to coordinate my x-axis with my y-axis and screwing it all up, all I can think of is how bad I've always been at math, how bad FDA wrote he is at math, how bad my dad has always been at math. Hell, my dad's so bad at math, he even has his accountant pay all his bills for him, because when he tries to balance his own checkbook . . . Well, let's put it like this: When my mom was still alive, she used to say to him, "Balancing your checkbook isn't an approximate art. It's an exact science. You're not supposed to just say, 'Who cares about a couple of thousand either way?'"

And all the time I'm thinking all of that, I'm totally sick to my stomach, and not just because I know I'm flunking this stupid pop quiz.

And now it's Tuesday, Tuesday night being our first real cheerleading assignment.

Of course, Farrin isn't the only other cheerleader on the squad. I don't want to give that impression. It's just that she *is* the squad captain. Plus, she is just so generally awful, it *feels* like she is the only other one. But there is also Belinda Sesame, a black-haired girl who is always eating some kind of seeds; Chathy James (that's not a typo; for some bizarre reason, she insists on spelling "Cathy" with a *Ch* and will get all weird on people when they wind up calling her, well, Chathy, as in *Chitty Chitty Bang Bang*), who has red hair; and Caitlin Cox, whose blond-haired, blue-eyed head would look normal enough, I suppose, were it not for the fact that she wears braces. Not that there's anything wrong with wearing braces, but each brace

Caitlin has—Cait to her inner circle—is a different color of pastel crystal: pink, purple, yellow, green. I'm pretty sure she doesn't have orange. It would be too gross if she had orange. Chathy let slip—meaning she actually talked to me, which I've kind of gotten the impression Farrin has forbidden the others to do—that Caitlin saw some girl with braces like those on *American Idol* and thought they looked cool. This made me want to go straight to Caitlin and say, *They're not supposed to be* jewelry. *They're just braces in your mouth. Just get it over with!* But I didn't, figuring I was already hated enough on the squad.

With Farrin and me, that makes five of us on the cheerleading squad. Well, of course, Waylord, even tiny Waylord, can afford to have more than five cheerleaders. I mean, five cheerleaders would hardly make much of a pyramid, would they? But I figured you'd just want to get a sense of who all is there besides Farrin and me. You don't really need to know every last name.

Actually, there *are* only five of us. I'm just getting carried away, trying to distract myself from my troubles by selling Waylord as being a bigger school than it is. But, nope, there are just us five: me; Farrin, who hates me; Belinda the Seed Girl (black hair); Chathy, whose name says it all (red hair); and Caitlin with the Claire's Accessories teeth (blond). This means that we have all the hair demographics covered—well, except for gray. And bald. In a way, we're kind of like Josie and the Pussycats, except Josie and the Pussycats were a band, their leader was a redhead and nice while Farrin is blond and not, and there were three of them to five of us. Plus, even if we were Josie and the Pussycats, there was still only a total of four girls on that show if you include the evil and conniving Alexandra Cabot—I think we can safely tap Farrin to be her—leaving me to be who exactly? Sebastian? *The cat?*

And Josie and the Pussycats had way cooler uniforms than we get to wear now. I mean, I'd much rather be wearing *"Long tails and ears for hats . . ."*

"D'Arc!" Farrin snaps. "What exactly are you doing?"

Shit. I hadn't realized I was doing that out loud.

"Look, D'Arc, if you're not going to take this seriously . . ."

"Jeez, Josie, er, I mean, Farrin, I'm just, you know, trying to get in the proper cheering mode, that's all."

Cheering for Waylord is kind of a depressing thing, so if I actually knew how to get in a mode and wasn't just faking it, this would be a good time to do that. Get in the mode.

"Long tails and ears for hats" would definitely be an improvement over the supertight ponytail I've got my hair gathered into. I have to do it this tight, I've learned to my horror during practice sessions, otherwise my hair just keeps coming out like there's a big electrical outlet somewhere just calling my finger's name, waiting to properly electrocute me.

"Doesn't it hurt your *brain*, D'Arc," Farrin says, "having your ponytail so tight?"

As a captain, Farrin is *such* an inspiration and role model.

"At least I don't have to think about you when my brain's squeezed so tight," I mutter under my breath.

"Did you *say* something, D'Arc?" she demands, her pom-poms firm on her hips like they're two guns, she's Jesse James, and I'm about to be made dead.

"I merely *said*," I say louder, smiling sweetly, "that I can't wait to cheer for you tonight."

She knows this isn't it. I can tell by her expression. But unless she wants to declare me a threat to national security and put a wiretap on me, she'll just have to accept it.

So there we sit, in the front row of the bleachers, waiting for the girls' team's game to be over before we go to work. We have to sit through the girls' game because it would be impolite not to. But we're not allowed to cheer for the girls' team because—get this!—we're supposed to save ourselves, our voices, our energies, our enthusiasm, and most especially our pom-poms for the boys' team. I mean, how sexist is that?

Behind us, filling the rest of the bleachers, are students from the school, plus lots of parents and teachers. Of course, my dad's not one of the parents in the stands. I didn't even bother telling him I was cheering tonight, just had Mohammed ride me over in the cab right after dinner. Attendance at sporting events at Waylord is practically mandatory. Given the small student body of the school, how would they ever fill the place if they didn't *make* people come?

And it's really depressing, sitting quietly in the front row, because the girls' team is *great*! T'Keyah throws in fifty points all on her own, setting some kind of record for private schools. Yet we're allowed to cheer her and the rest of the team on only in whispers, lest we not have enough throat left for the boys.

And it's even more depressing because when I look up at the rafters, I see championship pennants for the girls' team for the last five years straight, while for the boys' team I see nada, unless, of course, you count the one from the championship back in the school's founding year of 1917, which I personally don't.

And what's most depressing of all is that when the boys' team takes the floor, they just plain *suck*. Even with Jack out there on the floor, they still suck.

Well, okay, Marcus Dawson, T'Keyah's boyfriend,

doesn't suck at all, which she lets him know by sticking around to watch his game, shouting at the top of her lungs like a cheerleader every time he scores. And Jack doesn't suck either. I just wish that, instead of wearing those long and loose down-to-the-knees shorts like all the other players wear, Jack was wearing the supertight, supershort shorts my dad told me players used to wear when *he* was growing up. I would definitely like to see more of Jack's legs. But the other three guys on the floor playing for Waylord? Put it this way: Mouse is the best of the bunch—Mouse, who has morphed from Michael back into Mouse, as evidenced by the slooooooow way he moves his legs up and down the court. If it is possible to do a slooooooow-motion layup, Mouse is doing it. It's like he's practically stopped the videotape as he rolllllls up to the basket, jummmmps . . . and misses.

Still, Mouse and a dismal halftime score of 41–23 in favor of the other team, some all-boys' academy from Westport, can't dampen my enthusiasm for Jack as we take to the middle of the court.

"Jack, Jack, he's our man! If he can't do it, no one can!" I chant at the top of my lungs, pom-poms flying to beat the band. Well, if Waylord had a band.

"D'Arc," Farrin hiss-whispers from beside me. "Could you *be* any lamer? That's not even the cheer we're supposed to be doing."

Oops. Guess I got carried away with wanting Jack to be my man.

"Oh. My. God." Farrin continues to hiss-whisper. Then she turns to me, pom-poms on hips, getting right up in my face. "You *like* Jack, don't you?"

Double oops.

"Well, of course I *like* Jack," I hiss-whisper back, doing my own pom-poms-on-hips thing, backpedaling like mad all the while. "Why wouldn't I like Jack? Everyone likes Jack. I mean, come on, it's not exactly like he's *you*."

Triple oops. I'm thinking maybe that was the wrong thing to say. Maybe she'll punch me?

I put my pom-poms up in front of my face, to keep her from punching me. "Um, Farrin?" I say.

"*What?*" she snaps.

"Um, aren't we supposed to be, like, um, cheering out here?"

"Oh, yeah," she says, a dangerous gleam coming into her eye, "we're supposed to be cheering out here . . . *D'Arc.*"

Then she shouts to the rest of the squad, "*PYRAMID!*"

Shit. Shitshitshitshit*shit*. If there's one thing I hate most about all the things I hate about cheerleading, doing the pyramid is the thing I hate the mostest.

The pyramid, such as it is with only five squad

members, involves Belinda, Chathy, and Caitlin getting down on all fours on the floor to form the first tier. Then, even though Farrin is the tallest and strongest—meaning I think *she* should be on the bottom—Farrin by herself forms the second tier, probably because she's the only one with legs long enough to straddle her knees all the way from Belinda's to Caitlin's back; Chathy, the weakest link in the bottom, and thus in the center, doesn't have to bear any weight at all. Then, the way it works is, I'm supposed to step up the pyramid onto Farrin's back, since I'm the smallest and lightest, rising to my feet once I'm successfully on her back and spreading my arms wide in a big V. All this while shouting out some dumb cheer.

This is the way it's supposed to work, at any rate, the way it's always worked in practice. Sort of.

But it does not work this way on this night. Oh, no; on this night no sooner have I risen up on Farrin's back than she half rises up herself, rearing like an angry pony, tossing me off so hard that I fly backward through the air. Being the awkward bundle of noncoordination I am, I fall with a leaden thud—*thud!*—flat on my back.

Later, as the medical personnel on hand are looking me over—I swear I'm the only cheerleader in the history of Waylord, probably in the history of the world, to require medical assistance—I hear Farrin explaining that the reason she made that move was because there was a spider crawling up her leg.

Oh, yeah. Right.

Somehow, I doubt that. But with my head starting to pound—I can feel a lump rising at the back of my skull when I touch it—I am in no condition to publicly accuse her of what I am certain of: She did it on purpose.

"Be careful," I hear Jo-Jo say to the med tech. "She's one of my favorite students."

Well, that at least is nice.

And then another nice thing happens, the only really and truly supernice thing to happen in the whole sorry night. Jack kneels down beside me, puts his hand on the side of my face.

"Are you going to be okay, Ren?" he asks.

Wow.

I nod, no longer feeling the pain in my brain at all.

"Good," he says. Then: "*Man*, you flew off Farrin's back like a rocket shooting for the moon."

Ooh. I smile. I think he likes me.

And now it's Wednesday, and I'm allowed to skip cheerleading rehearsal to go home on the bus with Mandy Nicholas so I can be her mentor.

It's better than the last time because Mandy is starting to soften. She's not so bitter today about not having as much money as some of the other kids at Waylord, like me. And Mr. and Mrs. Nicholas seem to really be warming to me too, which will work out great if I ever get my way with their son. In fact, the only bad thing about going over to the Nicholas house this afternoon is that Jack's not in it, still being at school at basketball practice. It would be great if he were here. I mean, can't he just skip for once?

First thing when I wake up in the morning on Thursday there's an e-mail from Sex World saying I have a private message from FDA.

From: FDA
To: SexGurl1

We're all set for tomorrow night at 8:00. I've booked us Room 13 at the Starshine Motel, which I told you about on Rte. 6. The name it's booked under is "Fidoau," so don't forget you're supposed to be Mrs. Fidoau when you check in. Think that 13 might be our lucky number . . . ?

What the hell kind of name is Fidoau? It looks like it's missing a few consonants in there somewhere. Hell, I can't even pronounce it. Still, I guess that's not the point. Obsessing about it is only making me delay the inevitable. And even though I don't really want to, even though my skin is crawling, my stomach rolling the whole while, I force myself to write back.

From: SexGurl1
To: FDA

Oh, yeah. That sounds like our lucky number. . . .

And now it's Thursday afternoon, Thursday after school, Thursday after cheerleading and basketball practice. . . .

"*Euww!*"

That could just as easily be me or Kiki saying that, but it is T'Keyah.

I had called both girls up, asking if they would go shopping with me, help me pick out an outfit for an important occasion. Of course they assumed I must have meant the Sadie Hawkins Dance. T'Keyah suggested right away that we meet in their town of Ridgefield, where the shops are more exclusive. But I have to rely on the kindness of taxi drivers, and somehow, I don't think they will want to take me so far again, so soon after dropping me off and picking me up from Kiki's party last weekend. When I next saw Mohammed, he told me Helena had not been pleased.

It is Thursday night, after school and sports practice. It is the first time since I've moved to Danbury, the first time since I've started attending Waylord Academy, that I'm doing something socially with other girls outside of school; Kiki's party doesn't count because, well, so many other people were invited. If the world were a fair place, I would be allowed to be excited on such an occasion; but my world is no longer fair, and I am not.

I suppose I could have told them on the phone, probably should have told them, what this is all about, that it has nothing to do with the Sadie Hawkins Dance. But when I started to talk, the words froze in my mouth. The idea of saying *My father is a sex pervert* over the phone just seemed too icky, and I decided to wait, to play it by ear. Maybe, I thought, I would not tell them at all.

Now we are at the mall, and we are going through the stores: Express, American Eagle, Aldo. I find myself longing for Manhattan. "*New York is where I'd rather stay* . . ." Not to mention trying on so much ready-to-wear. How is a girl supposed to be an individual, no matter how fab the outfit, when there are dozens of each item in every size?

Still, I try to get myself into the spirit of things, try to convince myself that this is fun, that I am not doing this for the reason I'm doing this.

At first, as I stand in dressing room after dressing room, Kiki and T'Keyah bring me the kind of outfits that I would want to wear if I really were going to the dance with Jack Nicholas.

I reject them all, because, as I tell myself inside, *These are the kinds of things I would wear to attract a boy. But it is a man I am dealing with here.*

They are surprised at my rejections: "What's wrong with lots of gauze and fringe?" "How can spandex *not* be your friend?"

But I explain, without really explaining, that I need something that will attract a guy who is slightly older than the guys we are used to at school.

The look in their eyes changes now. I can see myself going up in their estimation. I can see them thinking, *Is Ren going to bring a college guy to the Sadie Hawkins Dance?*

It is all I can do to stop myself from saying, *Hey, that guy is no college guy. That guy is my father.*

But as they reverently bring me more mature items, as the pinstripes start piling up on the dressing room chair, I think of the FDA who wrote to SexGurl and SexGurl1—not thinking of him right now as my father, because it is just too icky to keep thinking that, but thinking of him objectively as the guy who wrote to Farrin and me—and I realize this is all wrong too. Undoubtedly, Farrin's chief appeal to FDA is that she *is* young, or at least much younger than he is. He will not want her to look like a lawyer. He will not want her to look like Hillary Clinton. He will want her to look like a teenage sex toy. He does keep mentioning wanting to see her in her school uniform; not to mention, out of it. Hell, he'd probably love it if she looked even younger, like, say, the Olsen twins about ten years ago, when neither was publicly anorexic yet.

So I ask Kiki and T'Keyah to bring back the gauze and the fringe, bring back the spandex.

Of course, by now they think I am fucking nuts.

At last, finally, we have a winner: For her undercover operation, Our Girl in School will be wearing distressed stretch low-riders that have a slight green tinge to them, which nicely echoes the gauzy top Kiki likes best. The green in the top is not like any green found in the natural world; it has undertones of gray. But the top itself has gold trim on the collar and bell sleeves, and it opens in a deep V, then opens again from the cleavage down. In fact, the top is only closed at all with a single gold elastic insert about the width of a woman's cleavage and about a half inch thick. There is a braided gold glitter tie that you use to make a bow in front of it. You can wear it sans bra or with. I will definitely be going for with, and I buy the matching gold-sequined bra so that I will not look like a sleaze with my regular bra inelegantly peeking out over the edge of the top.

Then I send Kiki and T'Keyah on ahead to the food

court to order us Diet Cokes and slices at Sbarro, using the extra ten minutes to stop off at a cheesy accessory shop, where I buy a long blond wig.

Clearly, I have thought of everything. If FDA—if *Dad*—arrives at the Starshine Motel and finds mild-mannered Ren D'Arc there, he might just be quick enough on his feet to concoct some kind of bizarre alibi to explain away the twisted situation. *Ha!* he might say. *Caught you! I always knew it was a mistake to let you keep a computer in your bedroom. I knew I should have kept it in the kitchen all along, where I could keep an eye on you. I just strung you along, waited to see how far you'd go in hanging yourself.* Actually, Dad would never say that last sentence. He has too great a command of the English language. Clichés and anything trite are just not him.

Omigod, I can't believe I'm defending this guy!

But, whatever, he definitely would say, if he were trying to divert attention from his own behavior, *Don't you know how dangerous it is, Ren, to meet strange men at motels? You could get hurt. If you're interested in having sex, I'll take you to the doctor for birth control pills myself. Hell, if you can't meet anyone you like, I'll throw a party and have all my friends bring their sons. But don't do it like this.*

Or something like that.

Anyway, this is why I need the wig: *If* I arrive early, and *if* I keep the lights down low, he will not see that it's me at first. He will think I am SexGurl; he will think I am Farrin. And I will be able to see, by the look on his face, what his first reaction to that person will really be.

And in that moment I will know whatever it is I need to know about my dad.

It takes me ten minutes more than the ten minutes I told Kiki and T'Keyah it would take me to get back to them, so I am ten minutes late when I finally sit down.

But I have used those ten minutes wisely. I have bought them each a pair of gold earrings shaped like wishbones. I have bought the same for each because I do not want one to get jealous of the other. In the event that I'd bought two different sets, one could have been deemed better than the other by the group.

Having two friends at once is definitely more complex than having none.

My mom always warned me that threes don't work in friendships and here I am defying her, trying to make three work against the odds because I like both Kiki and T'Keyah. Why should I have just one best friend, somewhere down the road, when maybe I can have two?

God, I wish Mom were still alive. If Mom were still alive, if she had not been crushed to death by Harry Potter, my dad would never have become a sex pervert. It is the death of my mother that has pushed him over the edge. I am sure of it.

Naturally, I used the AmEx Gold Card my dad gave me to pay for the clothes and the gifts. At first that didn't feel right. Should I be profiting off of—or, if not profiting, then enjoying the wealth of—a criminal? But then I realized two very important things: (1) I needed the clothes to lay my perfect trap; and (2) once my dad is taken off to prison or to rehab or to wherever he will have to go to recover from his illness, I will probably be sent to a foster home, where there will be no AmEx Gold Cards for me and where I will be forced to eat porridge and do my own laundry by hand, so I might as well enjoy the life I've grown accustomed to while I still have it.

T'Keyah and Kiki are thrilled with the gold wishbone earrings, even though they could easily afford them themselves with their own parents' gold cards. Well, it is always better to receive than to charge.

All this shopping and anxiety has made me hungry, and I'm halfway through the slice of pizza they've got for me before I start to talk.

"Could I talk to you guys about something?" I ask,

my mouth still half full of cheese and sauce and crust.

"Sure!" They both lean forward eagerly. In fact, they are so eager, I begin to doubt the wisdom of confiding in them.

I pull back.

"What is it?" Kiki asks.

"Is something wrong?" T'Keyah asks.

And now they look so genuinely concerned, I start to talk.

"Remember a while back," I say, "in Jo-Jo's class, when I gave my talk on, um, Austen?"

Now they look a bit disappointed. If all I am going to talk about is some stupid oral report I gave, they might as well be in Waldenbooks flipping through fashion and gossip magazines.

"It's not about the report," I say hurriedly. "It's about the reason I gave that report rather than the one I was supposed to give on Fitzgerald."

"That did seem weird at the time," T'Keyah admits.

"Yeah," says Kiki. "Not only did you switch subjects at the last second, but then you, like, did the whole thing off the top of your head. Who does such a thing? I mean, it was *really* weird."

I explain about the zebra notebooks with the hot pink feather handles and how I grabbed Farrin's off the lunch table instead of mine.

"*You* took Farrin's precious notebook?" T'Keyah says, her eyes going wide. "She doesn't let that thing out of her sight. You'd think she had all the bling-bling in the world hidden in that thing, the way she guards it so close."

"I didn't *take* it," I say. "I grabbed it by accident. I thought it was mine."

"I did always think it was weird," Kiki says, "you two having the same notebook and all. I mean, it's not like you have anything else in common."

I could point out that now that I've been to the Danbury Fair Mall with her and T'Keyah, I can easily see how two totally different girls can wind up with the same accessories. I mean, it's not like there's a whole lot of originality going on here.

But I have more important things to point out.

"The point is not Jane Austen or that Farrin and I have the same taste in notebooks," I point out. "The point is that, accidentally, thinking Farrin's notebook was my notebook, I opened it up, expecting to find my *Gatsby* paper inside."

"And what did you find instead?" T'Keyah asks. Then she says, "No, don't tell me. There *is* no light at the end of the green pier. Is that what this is all about?"

I look at her for a moment, and then I shake my head.

God, I think, *sometimes she's even weirder than I am.*

"No," I say. "This isn't about *Gatsby*, either."

"I know," Kiki says. "She has some silly, juvenile bullshit in there or something, right? Like little notes that say, 'Farrin loves Jo-Jo' or 'Mrs. Farrin Jones,' with dumb-ass little hearts dotting the *i*'s. Is that it?"

I think about my own zebra notebook, with my name linked to Jack Nicholas's, the dot in his *i* a dumb-ass little heart, and I hope these two never see it.

I shake that horrible thought off as well.

"No," I say, "she didn't have little notes like that in there, but she definitely had some little notes."

I explain about the e-mails, how there were so many of them, how I could tell they were written by a much older guy. I tell them about the Sex World website, the local chat room, about how I was worried about Farrin even after I returned her notebook, and how I logged on as SexGurl1 to see what I could see.

"You were worried about *Farrin*?" T'Keyah is shocked. "That girl's like Cockroach Doll or something. Come Armageddon, there'll just be the roaches and Jessica Simpson and Farrin left."

Weird. My mom used to say the same exact thing about Cher and Danielle Steel.

Some days there are just soooo many things to shake off.

"Well," I object, "but wouldn't she be surprised if she met FDA at some sleazy motel and wound up hacked to death and in little pieces!"

"FDA?" Kiki raises her eyebrows.

I explain how that's the screen name de plume of the sex pervert who was writing to Farrin.

"Omigod!" T'Keyah says. "The Federal Drug Administration wants to have sex with Farrin?"

"No, you twit." Kiki slaps T'Keyah on the shoulder. "That's the Food and Drug Administration." Then: "Omigod! The Food and Drug Administration wants to have sex with Farrin?"

And in that moment I remember why I wanted these two to become my best friends. They are more like me than they are different from me. Better, they make the same stupid mistakes. Sometimes.

"No," I say, "I'm pretty sure the Food and Drug Administration does *not* want to have sex with Farrin. To tell you the truth, I don't know why FDA uses that particular"—and here I remember the word my dad would use if he were discussing this—"acronym."

But, actually, I do know why he uses it. I just don't want to say. I can't say.

"Well," says Kiki, "I still don't know why you're so interested in saving Farrin. If there is one girl who can take care of herself, it's her. I mean, it's not like she'd be going to meet this FDA without knowing what was expected."

"Maybe I'm not so worried about Farrin," I say, "but what about other girls? I'm sure FDA wouldn't stop with just her, and then what? Maybe one day he'll attract some poor girl who doesn't understand what she's getting into."

"So?" T'Keyah shrugs. "Call the cops."

"Huh?" I say, sounding dumb, even to myself.

"Call. The. Cops." She enunciates each word as though I might be intelligence impaired, and maybe I am. "You still have the messages FDA sent you?"

I nod my head.

"So print them out," she says, "like Farrin did. Then take them to the cops and explain what's been going on. They'll be able to trace the ISP and find out who FDA is. Then they can arrest him for, I don't know, conspiracy to corrupt a minor or something. Even if they can't hit him with anything hard, at least he'll be on their radar and he'll know he is."

I'm shocked. Why didn't I think of that?

"I didn't think of that," I say.

"No?" T'Keyah looks mildly surprised.

"No," I say.

"Well, then, what was *your* plan?" she asks.

I explain how I agreed to meet FDA at the Starshine

Motel, how these clothes they just helped me pick out are for that, how I was going to spring a trap on him there, only I still hadn't figured out all the minor details.

"You *what*?" T'Keyah shouts.

"I told you I hadn't figured out all the minor details yet," I say defensively.

"Oh, well, by all means, take your time and call me when you do." Then she hits me on the shoulder, just like Kiki hit her a little while ago.

Now I am officially one of the group.

"You stupid moron," T'Keyah says. "This is nothing for you to be messing with on your own. Just call the damn cops."

I did not plan on telling them in advance. But now that we are here, now that I am living this moment, how can I *not* tell them? How can we ever become true friends, not just surface friends, if I don't trust them?

And I need friends, I realize, badly. I may not need to be loved by the whole world or even all of Waylord Academy—although, it would be nice—but I do need a few good friends. I need a few people I can talk to, trust. The time has come to unburden myself of my terrible secret. So I do.

That is, of course, when Kiki says, *"Euww!"*

T'Keyah's hand is over her mouth. I've always thought she's so much more sophisticated than me—

I mean, she has such superior hair—that it would be impossible for me to really do or say anything that would shock her, unless, of course, she was shocked at how bad I was at archery or basketball or how I was too stupid to figure out that if a problem involved X, Y, Z, and FDA, the solution was to call the PD so they could get the ISP and then put out an APB. God, there are way too many capital letters in my life right now.

But now T'Keyah is well and truly shocked.

And I realize then that my life is now well and truly fucked.

"Do you see now?" I say, almost begging. "Do you understand? I can't go to the cops over this. It's *my own father.* That's why I need to go there and trap him into admitting what he's been doing. Once I do that, I'll convince him to seek professional help."

"If he doesn't kill you first," Kiki says, looking scared on my behalf.

"He'd never do that," I say. "He loves me too much to do that. I know him, and that's not the kind of person he is."

"You used to *think* you knew him," T'Keyah says, speaking softly, "but look at where you are now." Then she reaches across the table and covers my hand with hers. Damn, her nails are nice. How does she pull that off and play basketball, too? "Hey, if I can help in any way . . ."

Before long, we wind down. I feel empty, like

there's nothing left to say. When I get up to leave, T'Keyah rises too, offering to come home with me.

"I thought you were coming home with me?" Kiki says, not like she's jealous or anything, just surprised. And it's true: Kiki drove the two of them here, they both live in Ridgefield, they'd naturally go home together.

"I just don't think Ren should be going back to . . . *that house* alone right now."

"But I can't come," says Kiki. It's nice to have a friend who, like me, also occasionally speaks with a slight whine in her voice. "I have a bio test to study for."

"S'okay," T'Keyah winks at her. "We promise we won't talk about you . . . *much*."

When we're all standing, I feel like I should say something. "Thanks," I say, "for everything. I swear, I don't even know why you guys would want to be friends with me. I mean, it's like even my *name* doesn't fit in."

"What are you talking about?" Kiki says.

"Well," I say, "look at the two of you. You've got unique names. You've got names that have the letter *K* in them. You're rare! Me, I've got a name composed of three of the most commonly guessed letters on *Wheel of Fortune*: R. E. N."

"The chick is weird," Kiki says, looking at T'Keyah.

"And *dumb*," T'Keyah adds. "Doesn't she realize

that the most commonly guessed letters *are* the most commonly guessed letters because they're the ones most likely to help you win?"

"Weird and dumb," T'Keyah and Kiki agree.

Outside, Mohammed thrills me by being on time for once—okay, maybe twice? three times?—and we wave good-bye to Kiki before hopping in the back of the cab.

"Miss T'Keyah," Mohammed says to her after I introduce them, "I am so glad to see Miss Ren has made some friends in Hat City. It is not good for a young girl to always be riding the O.K. Corral all by her lonesome polecat."

We try not to giggle.

"Wow, Ren," T'Keyah says, "so this is how you get around town? You cab it all the time with Mohammed?"

"Well, not just Mohammed," I say. "There's also George and Blue, but they have different shifts."

"Cool." She nods, as if she means it. "It's like you've got your own posse."

When we get to my house, we head right for the stairs, only to hear Mrs. Johnson call out, "Ren! Is that you? Dinner's in a half hour!"

T'Keyah raises her eyebrows at me. "Aren't you going to introduce me?"

We go into the kitchen, where Mrs. Johnson is cooking something that smells heavenly, something that smells of the islands. Mrs. Johnson always wears her jet hair in a twist held together with bobby pins. Her brown skin is smooth, looking at least ten years younger than her age, which is the same age my mother would be now. She always wears floral housedresses, an apron when she's in the kitchen, Nikes on her long feet.

"Are you staying for dinner?" Mrs. Johnson asks T'Keyah after welcoming her.

"No," T'Keyah says, looking like she's made a sudden decision. "Perhaps another time."

We head upstairs to my room. As soon as my door is shut, I turn to her.

"Thanks," I say.

"For what?" she says.

I don't know how to explain it, so I just say, "Just everything."

T'Keyah helps me hide my purchases away in the closet.

"I think I'm going to get going," she says afterward.

"Oh, no!" I say. "I thought you were going to stay longer."

"I did too," she says, then she looks embarrassed. "I'm sorry, Ren, but there's just something so *sad* in this house. I just gotta get out of here."

I'd feel offended by her words, but the thing is, I understand exactly what she's talking about: There *is* something sad about this house right now. Hell, if I felt I really had a choice, I'd be going with her. But there's stuff here I have to face. And, maybe, I have to face it alone.

"Will you be okay here tonight by yourself, Ren? Will you be okay here with just you and your dad?"

"Sure." I shrug, forcing a smile. "My dad's never hurt me in my life, never laid a bad hand on me. There's no reason to think he'll act any different tonight."

"Okay, then," she says. But then she just stands there as though she can't quite bring herself to go yet. "What time did you say FDA asked you to meet him at the Starshine Motel tomorrow night?"

"Eight o'clock," I say. "Right when the Sadie Hawkins Dance is starting."

"And that's when you're planning on getting there—eight?"

"No," I say.

"No?"

"No. I figured I'd get there at seven just to, um, you know, stake out the place, get myself ready. He said the reservation would be under Mr. and Mrs. Fidoau"—the name sticks like peanut butter coming out of my throat—"so I guess that's who I'll have to tell them I am: Mrs. Fidoau."

"Fidoau?" She laughs softly. "What an odd name."

"Yeah, well . . . Hey, the Sadie Hawkins Dance

is tomorrow night! Are you going with Marcus?"

"Absolutely."

I've been so obsessed with myself, I haven't even been thinking about anyone else.

"And is Kiki going with Michael Mouse?" I say.

T'Keyah makes a sour face. "Unfortunately."

"You don't like him anymore?" I'm surprised.

"Nah. He's not good enough for her."

"And what about Farrin?" Now I'm really trying to stall her departure. "Do you think she asked Jack?" Gee, do I sound really eager?

"Aw, who knows what that bitch is up to?"

"Yeah, I guess you're right."

"Okay, I'm really outta here now."

"But wait a second," I say. "Kiki drove you to the mall. How are you going to get back to Ridgefield?"

She whips her cell phone out of her pocket—God, she's got the coolest cell phone—and smiles as she holds it in the air, pointed toward heaven.

"I'm going to call Mohammed."

From: FDA
To: SexGurl1

You're not planning on backing out on me . . .
are you?

I spend the rest of the night avoiding my dad.

When Mrs. Johnson calls me for dinner, I say I am working on a school project and would prefer to eat in my room. Her hurt expression makes me feel bad for her, but I cannot bear the thought of sitting across the table from my father, behaving as though everything is normal.

My dad says I should not work so hard. Who do I think I am—him? He laughs. He says that I should be enjoying my youth while I still have it, that youth is a precious thing. When he says this, it is all I can do to keep myself from confronting him right then and there.

He offers to help with my project.

I tell him no.

He goes to kiss me on the cheek.

I turn away, tell him I am too old for that kind of thing.

I manage to avoid him the next morning too, then spend the day at school observing Farrin.

Remember earlier, when I said the day I went to New York to see Shannon, the night of Kiki's party, was the longest day and night ever? Well, ha! The longest day and night ever is *really* about to begin.

Farrin is changed Friday at school. She no longer looks filled with all the confidence that physical beauty and being paid attention to by everyone a person wants to have pay attention to them can give. She looks as though she's lost something, like she doesn't know where to find it.

I know why she looks like this. She hasn't heard from FDA in a long time and she no longer knows how to get in touch with him. She misses his attention. Having written to him myself, having known what that attention feels like, I can understand her loss. I remember how powerful I felt writing to him, how flattered I felt at what he wrote to me, before I realized he was my dad and the world turned icky.

Now she no longer has an older lover who writes her desperate letters. Now she is no longer special. She is just another teenager at Waylord Academy in Danbury, Connecticut.

But as the day goes on, I see her start to change back. I see her recover some of her old swing and swagger.

At first I don't know why, but later in the day I see her talking in the hallway to Jack Nicholas. And I realize this is it: She has asked Jack to the Sadie Hawkins Dance.

Oh, the price I have paid, oh, how much I have lost, because my father is a sex pervert.

After lunch on Friday, I am turning away from my locker, about to head off to Jo-Jo's class, when T'Keyah and Kiki stop me.

"You can't do this thing alone," T'Keyah says.

"We're going with you tonight," Kiki says.

I cannot believe they're doing this. True, I turned to them, but it was because I needed support and did not know where else to turn for it. It was not that I believed they thought of me as a real friend, not really. Still, I am touched by their concern.

"Thanks," I say, "but I have to do it myself."

"You shouldn't go alone," T'Keyah says again. "It's not right."

"Thanks," I say again, feeling more alone than I've ever felt in my life, "but it's my family. It's my problem."

It's not until T'Keyah and Kiki start to turn away that I notice they are both wearing the wishbone earrings I bought for them.

Jo-Jo's class takes my mind off my problems, at least for fifty minutes.

He is so funny, even when he is talking about Doyle.

It is like he knows how to talk so kids will listen and how to listen so kids will talk. I can easily see why Ms. Szarka, the art appreciation teacher, has such a huge crush on him.

Ms. Szarka is in her early thirties, red-haired, blue-eyed, and I suspect she does all her shopping at the sales rack at Petite Sophisticate. She also has rather large breasts, which I heard Mr. Welch refer to as "huge tracts of land" to the boys' soccer coach. The way I know she has a crush on Jo-Jo is that she was all upset when she heard Jo-Jo would not be co-chaperoning the Sadie Hawkins Dance with her and that Mr. Welch would be doing it instead.

Jo-Jo says something again about Doyle being "the father of the crime novel," and I see Farrin's hand shoot up.

We all look at her when Jo-Jo calls on her. It is so long before she says something, we are beginning to think she must be about to say something extremely important. Finally, she comes out with:

"I think fathers are just great." She smiles so hard at Jo-Jo, I think she is going to ask him to hook up with her right then and there. "Everyone should have a father," she says, "even a crime novel."

Clearly, between flirting with Jack first and now Jo-Jo, Farrin has gotten totally over FDA.

I see T'Keyah nod her head toward Farrin, rolling her eyes at me, and I wait for Jo-Jo to point out the obvious idiocy of Farrin's remark. But what I think will come doesn't come. Instead, he says:

"What an astute observation, Farrin, and how generous of you to make it."

Whoa, I think. This is taking talking so kids will listen and listening so kids will talk just a little too far.

Please don't encourage her, I want to tell Jo-Jo, *she will only say more stupid things.*

When class ends, I go to leave with everyone else when Jo-Jo stops me.

"Stay a minute, Ren?" he says.

It may sound like a question, but is it ever really a question when a teacher asks you to stay after class?

After the room clears out, Jo-Jo perches on the edge of his desk the way he likes to perch—one foot touching the ground, one dangling, arms lightly crossed.

"So," he says, "you seem to be adjusting nicely to Waylord. Are you having any problems?" He chuckles. "Everybody's always got at least one problem."

Oh, yeah, I've got a problem, a big problem, only I can't tell him about that, so I blurt out, "Farrin."

He chuckles again, a chuckle that turns into a full-out laugh.

"I'm not surprised," he says, after he's controlled

himself. "The Farrins of the world seem to wreak havoc wherever they go. If she were a literary character, Farrin would be Daisy Buchanan, Professor Moriarty, and Mr. Darcy all rolled into one."

"I guess," I reply, not really having a clue as to what the hell he's talking about.

I mean, of course I know who those characters are. But I have no clue why anyone would want to roll them together—they would make such a mess!—and I'm pretty sure if anyone did, the end result would *not* be Farrin.

"Hey"—he puts a hand lightly on my arm—"don't let her get to you."

"Okay." I mean, duh, what am I supposed to say? Am I supposed to burst into tears and cry, *But she's so mean!*?

"Good." He nods, as if agreeing with himself. "Good."

"Um, can I go now?" I say. "I'm kind of going to be late for art if I don't hurry, and, well, you know how Ms. Szarka is."

He chuckles again. "Sure," he says, "don't we all?"

Feeling released, I've got my hand on the door when he calls out to me. "Ren?"

I turn. "Yes?" I say.

"You make the Waylord uniform look good." He smiles.

"Um, thanks."

I go out the door, thinking it's great to have someone tell me I look good, even if it is a teacher. I'm actually smiling when I hear:

"Ooh, look, teacher's *pet*."

"Shut. Up." I speak to the owner of the voice, who is, of course, Farrin. She's slouched against the wall near the door to Jo-Jo's class, and it's only then that I notice Jack is with her. "So," she says, "teacher's *pet*, who are you going to the Sadie Hawkins Dance with tonight—Jo-Jo?"

I don't even answer her, barely look at Jack as I walk away.

Of course, I won't be going to the dance tonight. There will be no dance for me. I have other things to do.

On the bus ride home, everyone is buzzing about the big dance tonight, but Farrin and Jack are nowhere in sight.

"I think Farrin talked Jack into going to McDonald's with her after school," Mandy says when I plop down in the seat next to her at the back of the bus.

"Gee," I say, "they go to McDonald's a lot, don't they?"

"I know," Mandy says. "But if we're lucky"—and here she sniggers—"Farrin will clog up her arteries or maybe just blow up like a balloon."

I laugh. I can't help it, I like the Bratz doll.

"Hey," I say, hoping I sound more casual than I feel, "did Farrin ask Jack to the dance tonight?"

"You know," she answers, looking puzzled, "I don't know. I asked him who he was going with, but he wouldn't say."

"But he is going—right?"

"Oh, yeah. He's going."

Oh, crap.

I'm still thinking about the awful idea of Jack maybe going with Farrin, when Mandy interrupts my thoughts.

"I'm sorry, Ren."

"For what?" I say.

"I'm sorry about the hard time I gave you the first time you came to my house." She pauses. "And I'm sorry for what happened to your mom."

"Thanks," I say, meaning it.

"And hey." Her expression brightens. "I'd much rather have you wind up with Jack than that jerky old Farrin any day."

Well, at least there's that.

At home, I once again avoid my dad during dinnertime. Even though I am dreading what's about to happen in just a few short hours, I will be relieved in a way to get it over with. At least afterward I'll be able to go back to eating regular meals like a normal person. I mean, I don't want to die of starvation or anything over all of this.

"You've got to eat, Ren," Mrs. Johnson calls as she knocks on the door. I'm in my bedroom in my favorite pink, 100-percent silk, full-length bathrobe, trying on the long blond wig when she knocks. I quickly rip off the wig, shoving it under the bed before opening the door.

She's standing in the doorway, her hands holding a tray laden with pancakes drowning in syrup, fresh fruit, and a glass of fresh orange juice. There's even a single red rose.

"I know it's just breakfast food"—she shrugs, smiles—"but at least it's your favorite. At least it's something. I thought I'd just drop it off before heading on home for the weekend."

She juts her chin questioningly at my desk as if asking permission to place it down.

I nod.

She goes to leave after placing it on the desk, when suddenly I call after her, "Mrs. Johnson?"

She halts. "Yes?"

I hurl myself across the room and into her arms. A part of me knows I'm acting like the biggest geek who ever lived. But a part of me also feels like hers is the last kind face I'll ever see—*gulp*—alive!

"Thank you, Mrs. Johnson! Thankyouthankyouthankyou for always being good to me!"

"You're welcome," she says, clearly stunned and almost knocked over by my violent embrace. But as I hug her tighter, she slowly pushes out of my arms like a mouse escaping the squeeze of a boa constrictor.

"You eat your dinner now, even if it looks like breakfast," she says. "I gotta go."

And she scoots out the door before I can lunge at her again.

Well, who can really blame her?

I sit down in front of the pancakes, make a half stab at a piece—Mrs. Johnson has thoughtfully cut the stack up for me—but it feels too much like the last meal before my execution, and I'm just not hungry. Whether I want it to be or not, it's showtime.

Slowly, I slide into my new distressed stretch low-riders with the slightly green tinge, put on my gold-sequined bra, over which I put on the green top that is not like any green ever found in the natural world, with its undertones of gray and its gold trim on the collar and bell sleeves, with its deep V-neck and opening from the cleavage down, its single gold elastic insert spanning the cleavage, the gold glitter tie to make a bow. Usually, I love almost nothing more than wearing new clothes for the first time, but tonight it gives me no joy, and not merely because I got it all from some chain store at the mall. I put on strappy sandals, apply enough makeup to qualify me as a contestant on Tyra Banks's *America's Next Top Model* show, put my hair up in my high and tight cheerleader ponytail so it'll be easier to shove it up under the wig later on when I need to, then I toss the wig in my oversized glitter bag before surveying the results in the full-length mirror that hangs off the back of my bedroom door.

Except for the headache-inducing ponytail, I look really great, if a little trampy, even if it's only me saying so. The weight I've lost from not eating much lately, not to mention the cheerleading practices I've endured under Farrin's Simon Cowell–like regime, has left my stomach admirably firm beneath the revealing top. It's a shame that this whole look is being wasted on something so awful, when I'd much rather be doing something wonderful with it, like having Jack see me in it. It occurs to me that it makes sense, after all, that they make prisoners wear those orange jumpsuit thingies. If I were wearing one of those orange jumpsuit thingies, I might want to die.

I study my reflection one last time and realize it doesn't really matter what I look like, fashionwise. I just need to look old enough to be let into that motel, to be taken for "Mrs. Fidoau." I hope to God I do.

It's impossible to get out of the house without my dad seeing me, even though I do try.

"Going somewhere, Ren?" he calls out to me as I try to sneak past the living room to the front door, forcing me to turn back. He's sitting in a wing chair next to the unlit fireplace, flipping through the newspaper.

"Um, I didn't tell you I was going to the Sadie Hawkins Dance tonight?" I say.

"No, you didn't."

"Well, I'm going to the Sadie Hawkins Dance tonight."

He raises an eyebrow. "Dressed like that?"

I force myself to look like a normal bored teenager, speak to him with just the proper note of teenager-when-talking-to-parent disdain. "Everyone will be dressed like this," I say. "It's the latest thing."

He could object. I mean, I'm still a minor. He does pay for all my food, even if I don't eat it, and education, even if I don't like the school. But he doesn't seem to have the energy for objecting.

"Just make sure you've got your key," he says.

"Oh?" Now it's my turn to be surprised.

"Yeah, I was thinking of maybe going out myself tonight, go for a little drive just to get out of the house. I'm not sure what time I'll be back."

Well, of course he's going out tonight.

"I wouldn't want you to find yourself locked out," he says.

How considerate.

"Don't worry," I say, waving my oversized glitter bag with the blond wig inside it. Gee, I hope I've got my key in there too. "I've got it."

"Well, have a good time," he says, like he can't think of anything else to say to me.

"Yeah," I say, "you too."

Outside, Mohammed is blessedly on time. I asked him to be here at six forty-five, and there he is.

No sooner has Mohammed driven us out of sight of the house than I reach into the bag, pull out the wig, adjust it on my head.

"If it is all the same with you, Miss Ren," he says, eyeing me in the mirror, "I do not think I will offer to change headwear with you this evening. Somehow, I do not think I would look right as a blonde."

I stare out the window. Much as I like Mohammed, I am just not in the mood for small talk.

"May I ask where you are going dressed like this?" he says.

"I'm going to a dance," I lie. And then, I think, in a way, it's not a lie. This is a dance. The only problem is, it's a sick one.

"Then we are going to the school," Mohammed says, turning toward Waylord.

"No, no!" I say. Then I give him the address to where we're going.

When we pull up in front of the Starshine otel— the sign really does say "otel," since the *M* is burnt out—Mohammed looks upset.

"I am thinking this does not look like a good place for a dance, Miss Ren," he says. "Are you sure you have the right address?"

"Oh, no, no! I mean, yes, yes! Yes, I have the right address! But did I say dance before?" I chuckle nervously. "I don't think I said *dance*. I meant party! One of the kids from school rented out, um, a *suite* here, and a bunch of us are going to have a party. Just one big wholesome all-American party!"

Mohammed still looks skeptical. "I am not sure I like this. This place looks so . . . *seedy*." He's got a point there. The otel *does* look seedy. Who knew an *M* could make such a difference?

"It's just that sign," I say. More nervous chuckling. Before climbing out of the backseat, I go to pay him before he can object any further. Okay, I overpay him, my own form of payola. I should be on *The Sopranos*. "Really, it's all going to be fine. This is just, um, a cheerleading party. You know what a cheerleader is, right? Well, this is just a party with, um, five cheer-leaders. There's even going to be a mom there! And no alcohol or drugs, absolutely no alcohol or drugs. As a matter of fact, I think we're mostly going to just eat brownies and pray a lot."

Mohammed looks pointedly at my blond wig.

"Oh!" I put my hand on my fake hair. "But it's also a bit of a costume party too! Well, a wig costume party. Did I not already say that?"

Mohammed has mercy on me. Maybe he just can't stand to see me lie my way into the ground anymore.

"What time do you want me to come back to collect you, Miss Ren?"

Honestly. Was I supposed to have worked out *all* the details ahead of time?

"Not sure!" I say brightly, backing away from the car. Back away from the car, Miss, just back away from the car. "So, like, I'll call you!"

Then I run, or as best as I can run in my strappy high-heeled sandals, for the manager's office.

The inside of the manager's office—places like the Starshine otel, unlike The Plaza, do *not* have front desks with red velvet chairs guests can sit on while waiting for the bellhop to take their twenty-two pieces of luggage and French poodle up to their suites—is just as dingily depressing as the lacking-an-important-letter sign outside suggests. Looking up at the forty-watt exposed lightbulb with its pathetic pull cord dangling overhead, I feel like screaming at the unlit-cigar-chomping, red-haired lady behind the desk, *For God's sake, get a lamp shade!* But I'm sixteen years old, hoping to pass for legal, hoping this blue-eye-shadowed, heavy woman in all the mint polyester will give me a key to Room 13. So I figure now is maybe not the time to impose my superior sense of style upon the truly needy.

Not that I know what Scotch looks like, but I'd swear that's a full glass of it in the soiled water glass in front of her. And from the bleary look in her eyes, I'd swear it's not her first. The plaque in front of her says MRS. KILROY.

Well, of course.

"Fidoau?" I cough into my hand and say with what I hope sounds like more certainty than the first time, "I'm Mrs. Fidoau? My husband booked a room here? Room 13?"

She looks me up and down, then slowly swivels on her chair to look up at the Peg-Board behind her. The Peg-Board has twenty nails sticking out of it, each with a torn white piece of paper taped above it with hand-lettering: *1, 2, 13,* and so on. Dangling from most of the nails are two sets of keys, but a few of them have only one key. The nail for Room 13 has only one key.

"Huh," she says, reaching for it. "Looks like *Mr.* Fidoau got here before you."

Oh, shit, I think. Here I bother to take the precaution of getting here an hour early so I have time to mentally prepare, and FDA gets here *more* than an hour early?

"Funny, though"—she scratches her head—"I don't remember any *men* coming in here tonight."

I gaze pointedly at her Scotch, thinking, *Well, of course you don't.*

She gives me the key.

"No playing loud music, no fighting, no shooting up the room," she informs me. "Checkout's at eleven or you get billed another full night."

Then she goes back to reading a paperback book she's got flattened open on the counter. I read the title upside down: *Love Me or Don't Leave Me.* Well, my folks always said, so long as people are reading *something* . . .

I take the long walk—long because I walk there as slow as molasses—down to Room 13. I try the handle, taking a deep breath as I do so, figuring that maybe Mr. Fidoau just left the door open for me since he checked in ahead of me, but it's locked. Maybe he's some kind of safety freak? My hand shakes as I turn the key in the lock, slowly push the door open. Maybe I'm a safety freak now too. Certainly, I don't want any sudden surprises. The room is dark, the only illumination coming from the lights from the highway behind me. Immediately, I hit the switch just inside the door and swivel fast in a 180-degree turn like I'm practicing for a guest shot on *Law & Order* or something.

My eyes blink as I see . . . nothing. Well, of course there's furniture in the room—a double bed with a thin purple floral bedspread, a tiny night table that looks like it's made out of some fake wood with an orange-shaded gooseneck lamp on it and a phone that looks none too modern, a fake-wood chair with orange fake-leather cushions for sitting, and an old-fashioned TV suspended from the ceiling like in hospitals; all awful-looking furniture like nothing you'd ever want to spend time living with—but there are no people in it, no FDA. There are two closed doors, one I figure for a closet, the other for the bathroom. All the furniture has a thick layer of dust on it, and I don't even want to begin to think of what that bathroom must look like.

"Hello?" I call out nervously. "Anybody home? I'm he-re!"

When no one answers, I feel like an ass. Well, of course that Mrs. Kilroy in the manager's office must have made a mistake. I mean, she did say no men have come through tonight, right? Probably, someone else came for a different room, she gave them the key for 13 by mistake, and now that poor slob, whoever he or she is, is roaming all over the otel, trying to find the right room.

Sheesh.

I look at my watch: 7:15. There's still forty-five minutes left until disaster.

So what do I do? I sit down on the edge of the depressing bed and think of—what else?—Eloise.

I mean, you do know who Eloise is, right? The Kay Thompson series about the little six-year-old girl who lives in The Plaza Hotel with her nanny? As a little girl, I loved those books. Not because I really loved Eloise; I mean, I always got the feeling that if she lived next door, I'd want to slap her. And it wasn't because I really loved the writing, which often flew right over my pretty little head. Of course, I did love that she lived in New York City, like me; well, except for when she went to Paris and Moscow. And I really loved that she lived in The Plaza Hotel, which was where I wanted to live.

But that wasn't it.

What it was, see . . . Oh, God, this is so hard to confess. It makes me look small. But, okay. Here goes. What it was, see, was that her mother didn't pay any attention to her at all! Oh, sure, Eloise got to live in really cool places and use room service all the time and make grown-ups wait on her, but her mother was never there! And I loved that, not because I wanted my mom not to be there, but because my mom *was* there. She was there, reading to me every day, putting Band-Aids on my skinned knees—not that I skinned too many—and tucking me in at night. Eloise's mom wasn't there for her, but my mom was always there for me, and my mom's thereness, when compared to Eloise's mom's lack thereof, made me feel *good*.

Does that make me, like, the smallest person ever, to admit that? I mean, come on. It's not like Eloise is a real person. She's a character *in a book*. It's not like I was taking comfort in one-upping a real person, like, say, Little Orphan Annie.

But enough about Eloise, for whom I suddenly want to wish nothing but the best. If it was showtime before, now it's do-or-die time.

The element of surprise may not have worked against me before, I think, but maybe now it can work for me now. I switch out the light and sit, waiting, in the dark.

Knock, knock!

"*SexGurl1*," I hear a voice urgently whisper from the other side of the door. The voice is not familiar, but then, these are not familiar circumstances to be hearing a voice. *"SexGurl1, open up! I don't have a key!"*

See? I was right. Mrs. Kilroy did give the key to the wrong person. Or lost it.

Gosh, it doesn't feel like I've been waiting in here for a whole hour.

I tiptoe over to the curtains, hold my wrist up to the gap so I can use the light from the moon outside to see the dial on the face of my pretty Fossil watch. Gee, this watch is pretty. I'd like to stare at it forever rather than answer FDA's hissed summons and open the door. And—oh, no!—it's only seven forty-five. FDA is fifteen minutes early, drat his overeager butt.

I'm not ready! I'm soooo *not* ready!

Yes, this watch sure is pretty. . . .

"SexGurl1! Come on! Are you in there?"

Once I let the drape fall down and start walking toward the door, the room is so dark that I can't see a thing, and I bang my shin against the bed.

Ouch.

Playing blind-girl's bluff, I walk awkwardly with my hands thrust out in front of me until I feel the door. I fumble my hand to the doorknob, give it a quick twist, yank open the door, and duck behind it so that I'm wedged between the door and the wall.

The light from outside casts FDA's long shadow on the carpet as he enters the room.

"SexGurl1? Are you in here?"

I'm still holding tight to the knob when his hand snakes around and grabs on to the edge of the door, prying it from my death grip and closing the door behind him.

Trapped.

"So, you're hiding back there," he says, still whispering but no longer hissing. "Playing possum with me, huh? Well, I like a little resistance."

It's like I can hear the smile in his voice. Suddenly, I feel stronger than I did a moment ago. I'd like to wipe that smile right *out* of his voice.

But my own confidence sags as quickly as it rose once I feel a hand on my arm, gently but firmly pulling me from out of my hideaway behind the door.

"Come here," he says. "I've been waiting for this moment for so long."

Then he takes me into his arms in what can only be described as a bear hug.

His hair against my cheek as he bends over to hug me feels thicker than my dad's. That's odd. Maybe he thought to wear a wig too?

At first I'm totally skeeved out. But then I tell myself: *Dad has hugged me a million times in my life, right?*

There's no harm in just a hug. And my dad can't help himself. He's just a sick monster, badly in need of extensive psychiatric help. Or maybe a straitjacket. And—the biggest "and" of all—in a minute this will all be over with. He'll realize it's me, the game will be afoot, and then I can get him the help he so desperately needs.

God, though, I hope he doesn't kill me first.

FDA's hands move from my back to my arms, snake their way up to my hair, which he caresses lightly, then grabs on to, tight. Even though I can't see his face at all, something kicks in, some other sense—maybe it's like blind people who hear better or deaf people who can feel the vibrations of someone walking toward them through the floor?—because suddenly, I'm sure he's lowering his face toward mine, getting closer with every second. I feel his breath on my face and realize that, with just one more tick of the clock, he's going to kiss me.

"Hey!" I say brightly, jumping backward out of his embrace. "How about we get some lights on in here?"

"Cool." I hear him chuckle. "You want it with the lights on? I *like* it with the lights on."

I stumble to the night table, banging my shin on the side of the bed again, and grope around until I find the switch for that hideous goosenecked lamp.

The light is so sudden after the prolonged dark, so

horribly fluorescent, I'm rubbing at my eyes as I turn around and see the man who has been in this room with me, the man who is also rubbing at his eyes. . . .

"Jo-Jo!" I scream, jumping backward.

"Ren!" he screams back, jumping backward too. Then he takes a step toward me.

I start to back slowly away from him, still in shock, but all I hit up against is wall. The door, the door to get out, is all the way on the other side of the room. He's between me and it, and it might as well be a mile away.

"What are you doing here?" I laugh nervously.

"I could ask you the same question." He chuckles, takes another step toward me. "You know," he says softly, "it's funny, but I always assumed it was Farrin to whom I was writing at Sex World. And then, when I got here tonight and felt those long soft tresses, especially at first when you turned on the light and all I could see was the blond hair, I was certain. But this"—and now he's standing right in front of me—"the fact that it's *you*, innocent you, makes it all just so much . . . *better*."

"Um, uh . . ."

"I've always liked your hair, Ren. But, I must confess, the blond wig is just so much more . . . *kinky*."

Like it's not kinky enough already? I think, ducking under his arm as he reaches for my fake blond mane.

I try to make a run for the door, but I'm no match for him in speed. I mean, hel-*lo*! Have you not noticed how short my legs are? He catches me from behind, wrapping his arms around my waist so tight that my feet come up off the ground. I try to kick back at him, but all he does is laugh at my ineffectual efforts.

"Ooh," he coos, *"feisty."*

Then he picks me up in his arms and throws me on the bed. "This just keeps getting better all the time," he says.

Then he's lowering himself on top of me. It's like watching a slow-motion sequence in a horror flick. At last, shaking my head to snap myself back to this awful reality, I open my mouth to scream, but I never get a chance to. Scream, that is. Because Jo-Jo puts his hand over my mouth, tight.

"You don't want that idiot in the manager's office, that lamebrain who couldn't even find the second set of keys to this room, to hear you, do you?" he says.

So what do I do right then? What would you do?

I bite down on his hand, hard, exercising the full force of thousands of dollars' worth of orthodontia. I bite down, and I won't let go.

"Ouch!" he screams.

Who's screaming now?

"Ouch!" he screams some more.

Over the volume and repetition of his screams—I'm holding that bite hard and refuse to let go—I hear something else.

"Monster!" I hear T'Keyah's voice scream, and look over Jo-Jo's shoulder in time to see her come charging out of one of the room's two interior doors. Maybe the bathroom?

"You . . . you . . . you you you . . . *English teacher*!" And this time it's Kiki's voice screaming as she lunges out of the other door. Maybe the closet?

"Wait a second," I say, releasing Jo-Jo's hand from between my teeth. "How did you two get here? And, by the way, if you were here all the time, *what took you so long*?"

Jo-Jo takes the opportunity to get off of me, making for the door. But in a flying tackle more worthy of a football player than a basketball player, T'Keyah leaps onto his back even as he's walking, wrapping her long legs around his waist from behind as she puts him in a choke hold and Kiki throws herself at his ankles.

"We blew off the dance!" T'Keyah shouts.

Wow. For me?

"But we wanted to wait until he did something incriminating enough to get him arrested before showing ourselves," Kiki says through gritted teeth.

Tough as my friends—my friends!—are, Jo-Jo is

still a man, an adult man, and a strong and desperate one at that. So, despite their tenacity, he pulls them both along with him by inches as he makes his way to the exit door and escape beyond. I can bet what he's thinking: If only he can get away, who's anyone going to believe—a respectable schoolteacher or a crazy girl in a wig and her two wild-haired friends? And, as a result of the struggle, they do look wild haired. Certainly, if I were a proper authority, I'd have trouble granting credibility to anything they said right now.

They're almost at the exit door, and I've just gathered my wits about me enough to join in the attack, making a lunge for Jo-Jo's knees—always go for the knees, right?—when that door bursts open from the other side too.

"God!" Jo-Jo yells, trying to take a step backward, despite the weight of now three girls restraining him. "What *is* it with the doors in this place?"

But who cares what the English teacher has to say?

Because the cavalry has arrived.

The cabdrivers are here.

And there, framed in the doorway, in all their cab-driving glory, is my posse: George, Mohammed, and Blue.

"Get your hands off Miss Ren," Mohammed demands.

Well, technically, he's wrong. It's not Jo-Jo who has

his hands on us. It's T'Keyah and Kiki and I who have our hands all over him.

"This is a tire iron," Blue announces, tapping the metal thing she's gripping in one hand menacingly against the palm of the other.

"Yeah," George says, "and she knows how to use it."

"No!" Jo-Jo screams as Blue steps toward him. "No! Please! Not in the face!"

He must be screaming pretty loud, because no sooner is the last scream out of his mouth than Mrs. Kilroy, the woman from the manager's office, appears in the doorway. She looks at me accusingly. I'm still holding tight to Jo-Jo's knees. "Hey," she says, "didn't I tell you I won't tolerate any trouble here?"

I guess even the Starshine otel has its standards to maintain.

Then she calls the cops.

While we all wait for the cops to arrive, I look at Mohammed, leader of my saviors.

"How did you know to come back?" I say.

"I knew about it all along," he says. He nods at T'Keyah. "She told me, when I drove her home last night."

"And Mohammed told us," says George.

"We couldn't let you do this alone," says Blue.

Wow. What can I say? These three are worth every excessive tip I ever gave them. They're worth their weight in gold.

Then lights flash outside, and before another minute passes, cops are in the room.

They arrest Jo-Jo, then they tell us we'll need to come down to the station to make a statement.

Once again, Mohammed comes to my rescue.

"Can it not wait until tomorrow?" he says. "Do you not see how much they have all been through already? They are just schoolgirls."

Truthfully, Jo-Jo looks a lot more the worse for wear than we do, but the cops concede Mohammed's point.

They go to leave, Jo-Jo in handcuffs between them.

But I have just one question before they take Jo-Jo away, something that's been bothering me.

"Why FDA?" I say. "Why did you go by FDA?"

"Fitzgerald," he sneers. "Doyle. Austen."

A lightbulb goes on over my head: FItzgerald. DOyle. AUsten.

Fidoau.

FDA.

The gymnasium at Waylord Academy sure looks better than it does when I'm cheerleading, the whole place festooned with little white lights like a house tastefully decorated for Christmas or something.

After the police led Jo-Jo away, T'Keyah and Kiki realized the Sadie Hawkins Dance would still be going on, that we all needed something pleasant after what we'd just survived, and so they drove over in Kiki's car while Mohammed drove me himself, promising he'd be waiting for me afterward, my own personal chauffeur.

When Mohammed pulled up to the entrance, T'Keyah and Kiki were already standing there. "Ready to go in?" they said.

I took a deep breath, nodded. After what we just went through, how bad could this—my first dance at Waylord—be?

And now we're inside, admiring the pretty lights, feeling the beat of the music thumping through the high-polish boards of the basketball court.

"Hey," T'Keyah says, "there's Marcus over there. Do you mind if I go over and say hello?"

From the look on her face, I can tell that if I say, yes, I do mind, she'll stay with me, but I don't want to hold her back.

"It's okay," I say. I point with my chin, smile. "Go."

Then Kiki says, "Ooh, there's Michael. Do you mind if I . . . ?"

I look over at Mouse. It's tough to see from that

distance if he's stoned or not. Kiki seems to read my mind.

"Even if he is," she says with a laugh, "at least he's *my* stoner."

"Go," I say, smile.

And then I'm standing by myself, all alone, looking at everyone else engaging in just plain old-fashioned high school fun all around me. It may not be New York City—New York City!—but it still looks pretty good to me.

Then I think of what tomorrow will bring, newspaper headlines screaming that Jo-Jo has been arrested for being an online sex predator, and I go cold inside.

I think of how all these kids, my classmates, will feel about this. Everyone was in love with Jo-Jo. Okay, maybe not the boys; the boys all resented him, but they'll still be shocked. And the girls really were all in love with him.

Regardless, whether boys or girls, it'll be a blow to them all. Their teacher, a well-respected teacher, is a criminal, and a really slimy one at that.

They'll go through the stages of grief, just as I have done since Mom died: denial, anger, depression, and some other stages in between. Somewhere in there, they'll start looking for someone else, other than Jo-Jo, on whom to blame all this, and they'll probably settle on me, once news of my involvement gets out. But I can handle that, especially since I know eventually the stages of grief will lead them to acceptance.

It is hard, even as close as I've been to this case, even with my relief that my father is not the guilty party, for me to grasp that it's Jo-Jo who was behind it. I liked him as much as anybody. And it's a threat to trust, the idea that someone in a position of such power who was so admired can do such a thing. And yet I know people are not always what they seem and that just because someone looks good on the outside doesn't mean they can't be bad on the inside.

It would be so easy, after this, to become suspicious of everyone, seeing shadows everywhere. But that's no way to live. Does Jo-Jo's being the bad guy mean that we can trust no one? No. I think it just means we can't trust Jo-Jo, and, more than anything else, it means that kids shouldn't be hanging out in sex chat rooms. That's what it means.

But it's too overwhelming, thinking all these thoughts in this moment, and I sneak out of the dance and find my way to the bathroom. Once there, I splash water on my face, leaning on the edge of the sink afterward. I look in the mirror and I look older to myself than I did when I left the house earlier this evening.

I hear a toilet flush, and in a minute Farrin is at my side, washing her hands.

"Did you just get here, *D'Arc*?" she says in her usual snide fashion. "I was beginning to think, hope, you wouldn't come."

Funny, but Farrin's snideness doesn't bother me at all anymore. Maybe it's because I know she'll wake up to the same bad news the rest of Danbury will tomorrow, that she'll be just as crushed as everyone else, even more so because she really did have a big thing for Jo-Jo. And she doesn't deserve that. None of us does.

"Even I have to get out of the house sometimes," I say to Farrin with as cheery a smile as I can muster. And then I add with a sincerity I feel, "If I don't see you later, have a good night."

Then I leave, letting the door close gently behind me.

I go back out on the basketball court, where I see T'Keyah dancing with Marcus, Kiki dancing with Mouse.

"Ren?"

It's Jack.

He looks so good in his jeans and black button-down shirt. I mean, it's just jeans and a black button-down shirt, but on Jack it looks good.

"Jack!" I say.

Well, that was brilliant. Of course he knows he's Jack. So I try something equally lame.

"Why aren't you with Farrin?" I blurt.

"Why would I be with Farrin?" he counters. Then he shrugs. "I felt like coming by myself tonight. I guess no one I wanted to be asked by asked me. Even though it's Sadie Hawkins and the girls are supposed to ask the guys"—he shrugs again, hands deep in pockets—"do you want to dance?"

I nod, let him lead me out into the middle of the dance floor.

We start to dance.

We're not even a minute into it, though, when he notices something.

"Hey, your shirt," he says, reaching out, touching a large tear in one of the bell sleeves that I hadn't even noticed was there. It must have happened during the struggle with Jo-Jo.

"Huh," I say. "I must have caught it on something."

It's not really a lie, and I'm just enjoying myself too much in this moment. It's like I'm Superman and he's Lois Lane, not having a clue as to what I've been up to in my alternate-universe existence. Just for tonight I want to keep it that way. By this time tomorrow Belinda and Chathy and Caitlin and Farrin, not to mention Jack, and everyone else who is and isn't here tonight will know what happened earlier. But that time is not here yet, and I just want to keep on enjoying this moment.

With Jack.

The dance ends.

"I'd offer to drive you home," Jack says. We've been dancing all night long, it seems. "But I don't have a car."

"That's okay," I say, smile, "because I do."

Mohammed is waiting outside, holds the back door open as we slide in, says, "Ah, Mr. Jack, it is my complete and utter pleasure to meet you."

At my house Mohammed waits in the cab to drive Jack on to his condo as Jack walks me to the door.

"I, um, had a great time with you tonight," Jack says.

"Thanks," I say. "Me too."

"So, look, maybe we can do it again sometime?" He blushes under the porch light. "I don't mean the Sadie Hawkins Dance. I mean, we *could* go to the Sadie Hawkins Dance again, maybe together next time, but that's not until next year." More blushing. I never noticed before what a blusher Jack is. "But maybe we could do something else another time? Or maybe we'll just see each other in school on Monday? Or maybe I could just call you tomorrow? Oh, hell," he says, lowering his face to mine and kissing me full on the lips.

It's a pretty damn good kiss.

And then Jack's running down the walkway to where Mohammed is waiting. He turns once and waves, yells, "So, okay, yeah, I'll call you tomorrow!"

I laugh, and then he's gone.

And so ends the really and truly longest day—and night!—ever.

But not quite. . . .

Shit.

I can't believe I forgot my key!

I push the doorbell, and when there's no answer, I start pounding on the door, louder with each pound, the stress of everything—good and bad—finally catching up with me.

"Ren?" My dad opens the door. He's got a bathrobe on.

"Dad!" I fall into his arms.

It feels so good to be there.

I don't know why I even open it. I've been ignoring her e-mails for days now. Maybe it is because the subject field of this one says something different. The others all said something along the lines of "Please open me!" or "Penis Enlargement Pill with Vicodin Chaser"—I guess she was trying to be funny—or even, simply, "SORRY!" But this one is different. There is something very humble about the "I was wrong" I see before my eyes.

From: Shannongirl@yaahoo.com
To: RenD@aaol.com

Ren, my old best friend,

Where do I start? It was wrong of me to take up with Todd in the first place. I mean, I knew you were still getting over him. And I didn't even really like him that much myself. Maybe it was just that I've always secretly been a bit jealous of you? I mean, your parents were always so cool. They had cool jobs. They cared so much about everything you did. Me, all I've ever had is a dad who's never home and a mom, well, you know what Stella's like. If it doesn't come in a Jimmy Choo box, she's just not interested. So maybe I did it so I could have just a little bit of something you had? But I know that's no excuse. There is no excuse. Anyway, here's the thing: I've broken up with Todd. Just so we're clear on this: I broke up with him; he didn't break up with me. If you don't believe me, you can e-mail him and ask him. We both know Todd's too stupid to lie.

Anyway, I'm sorry for the way I acted. I'm sorry for what I did, and not just because I got caught, but because I was wrong. I hope everything is going okay for you in Danbury. I'll bet you're making lots of friends. Are you still interested in that guy Jack? If so, how are things going with that? And how's your dad doing?

Most of all, I want to say that I'm not just sorry about hurting you with Todd. I'm also sorry I wasn't there for you more when your mother died. You needed me, and I just wasn't really there. I think it was because I didn't know how to be. Again, that's no excuse, but it is the way it was, and I'm sorry.

I really hope we can be friends again somehow, even if maybe we can never be best friends. I really hope it happens, more than anything, but I'll understand if you just can't.

Anyway, I think we can agree on one thing: Anything that's wrong with the world can almost always be laid at the feet of someone named Todd. ☺

Your friend, for life, whether you want me or not,
S

Who knew Shannon had such an e-mail in her? I guess in a certain way I'd been just as bad a friend as she had, never giving her enough credit, assuming she lacked depth. No, come to think of it, that wasn't as bad as her knowingly going after a guy she knew I liked, but it still wasn't as good as you'd expect from a friend.

I decide to write her back.

From: RenD@aaol.com
To: Shannongirl@yaahoo.com

S,

Thanks for the e-mail. Things are better in Danbury than you might think, given that it's not New York.☺ And my dad is doing better than he has been in a long time; I am too—thanks for asking. So much has been going on here, I don't even know where to start, plus I think my arms would fall off if I tried to tap it all out. ☺

About being friends again: I'm not sure how far we can go, but I'm willing to try. I'm willing to start again. Right now, though, I really need to go talk to my dad about something.

Thanks again for writing. Talk soon.

Love,
R

I knock on my dad's office door. I don't really want to disturb him when he's working, work being the only thing that seems to make him feel better. But how can I get his attention, how can I talk to him, if I don't disturb him?

"Yes?" I hear his voice call. "Come in?"

I open the door, and there he is, working in front of his computer on some book. He looks up at me over his glasses, and when he sees it's me, he smiles, really smiles, like he hasn't since before Mom died.

"Dad?" I say.

"Ren?" he says back with a laugh, like we're introducing ourselves to each other for the first time.

And all I can think of is all the times he let me disturb his work when I was young, how good that made me feel, how safe, how loved.

"I was just wondering . . . ," I say.

"Yes?" he says.

"I mean, I know you're probably busy and everything, but I was just wondering if maybe we could do something, do something together today?"

"Like what?"

"I don't know." I shrug. And I don't know. I guess I haven't really thought this out. "Movie, maybe. Lunch. Ice cream."

"It's kind of cold for ice cream."

"You're right. I guess I just thought we could do something together for once," I say lamely. I start to leave the room, start to pull the door shut behind me, mumbling, "I guess you're too busy. . . ."

"Ren?"

I stop. I turn around. "Dad?"

He smiles at me—a wide, happy smile, not a sad one.

"Ice cream sounds perfect," he says. "Get your coat."

"Okay." I look down at the shorts I've been wearing, since it's plenty warm in the house. "Um, maybe I should put on pants first too."

I race up the stairs to my room, exchange my shorts for some Juicy Couture sweats. Watermelon colored, just in case you need to know. Then I sit down at my desk and take the time to do one last thing before rushing back down to meet my dad, who still doesn't know that before we go get that ice cream, we're going to have to make a *lit*-tle stop at the police station. Gee, I hope my dad won't be too pissed at me.

I know they won't put Jo-Jo away for life for what he's done or anything drastic like that, but at least they'll probably put him in prison for a while, get him proper psychiatric help, put him on a watch list of predators, and I'm positive he won't be working anywhere like Waylord ever again, around kids, which is an excellent thing.

When you can't get things perfect, sometimes you have to settle for enough.

But I don't have any more time for Jo-Jo now, don't want to waste any more time on him. My dad is waiting, and I have just this one thing left to do:

Dear Mom,

Thanks for everything. Thanks for always being there for me, all the days of my life, even now. Thanks for always living in my head and in my heart.

You can stop worrying about me now,

because I know, wherever you are, you still worry about me. You always did. But you can stop now. You can let go if you need to.

Remember that thing I told you about there being a problem with Dad? Well, it looks like it was a false alarm. It's weird. I had this idea that Dad was doing something bad, something really bad, and I think I was so quick to believe that because, well, I think that for the longest time a part of me blamed Dad for your death. I was so busy looking for someone to blame I even blamed J. K. Rowling! Isn't that the craziest thing you've ever heard? Of course it wasn't her fault. It was just a freak accident, even if it did involve her books. But still, I couldn't accept it. I had to have someone to blame for it, and when I wasn't busy deluding myself into believing it was J. K. Rowling's fault, I blamed Dad. Why couldn't someone save you? Why couldn't _he_ save you? But I realize now how wrong I was. Sometimes bad things happen because some people are evil. But sometimes bad things happen simply because they just do.

Anyway, I think Dad's going to be okay now; he's going to be just fine—_we'll_ be fine together. We'll take care of each other.

Oops, I almost forgot! I've finally made some friends here in Danbury, some really good friends. And remember I told you about liking Jack? Well, it looks like maybe, just maybe, things are going to work out for me with him. Maybe. So cross your fingers for me, Mom!

Okay, more about Jack and everything else later, the next time we talk, always more later.

Love, always love,
Ren

Author's Note

It may seem unlikely that predator and prey would be in the same school, as depicted in my novel, but let's take a look at some facts provided to me by Adam Van Auken, director of technology at Wooster School. The following link, http://www.netsmartz.org/stories/../media/teresa-300k.asx, will take you to something called "Tracking Teresa." It shows what a predator, posing as a fellow chatter, can discover in just a short time after identifying potential prey in a chat room. By starting with basic profile information, within eight minutes the predator knows Teresa's first name, approximate age, interests, e-mail address, IM account, time she's likely at home, and phone number. Within just twenty minutes the predator knows Teresa's full name, full names of her family members, her address, directions to her house, and the school she most likely attends.

Be smart. Be careful. Be safe.

Acknowledgments

Thanks to the professionals: my agent, Pamela Harty, and all the other helpful people at the Knight Agency; my delightful new editor, Sangeeta Mehta; assistant editor, Siobhan Wallace; publicist, Lila Haber; and the whole S&S team . . . who even sign their own holiday cards! Special thanks to Julia Richardson for starting with me on this path.

Thanks to the invisible friends: the online communities at Backspace and MySpace for adding so much to my life.

Thanks to the visible friends: Sue Estabrook, for reading early drafts and always making me better; and the members of the Friday Night Writing Group—Andrea Schicke Hirsch, Greg Logsted, Robert Mayette, Krissi Petersen, and Lauren Catherine Simpson—for bolstering above and beyond.

Thanks to the family: the extended family, of course, and in particular my irreplaceable mother, Lucille Baratz; my irreplaceable husband, Greg Logsted; and my irreplaceable daughter, Jackie Logsted—there simply are no other useful words for that which cannot be replaced.

Thanks to readers everywhere.

About the Author

Lauren Baratz-Logsted is the author of seven books, including the critically acclaimed *The Thin Pink Line*. Her first novel for young adults, *Angel's Choice*, was praised for its "vivid portait of the dark side of fleeting hookups and teen pregnancy" by *SLJ*. *Kliatt* says, "Readers will be changed by the total reading experience." Lauren Baratz-Logsted lives in Danbury, Connecticut, with her husband and daughter.

What if you could see your best friend's dreams?
How about your crush's?
Or a stranger's?

YOUR DREAMS ARE NOT YOUR OWN

WAKE

LISA McMANN

She can't tell anybody about what she does—
they'd never believe her, or, worse,
they'd think she's a freak. . . .

From Simon Pulse
PUBLISHED BY SIMON & SCHUSTER